"Lucas, I see an island." The fortune-teller exhaled smoke slowly from her cigarette. "An island. Small. Maybe nearby this place." She held up her hand and slowly gestured in a huge circle. The bangles fell abruptly down to the bottom of her wrist, tinkling loudly. Lucas flinched. If the fortune-teller noticed, she didn't show it. Instead she looked past him and blew three perfect smoke rings that floated over his shoulder and disintegrated.

"An island. A man is there. Older. Traditional. Your father?" She glanced at him, her eyebrows raised.

"Yes, my father," Lucas croaked.

"Your future is this man's future. You will never leave this island. You are destined to the island. Do you understand me?"

Lucas gasped. Had he expected this? He felt as if he had been hit by a rock. Deep down in his heart he realized suddenly he'd known all along what the fortune-teller would say and why. His worst nightmare had come true.

Don't miss any of the books in
Making Out
by Katherine Applegate
from Avon Flare

#1 ZOEY FOOLS AROUND
#2 JAKE FINDS OUT
#3 NINA WON'T TELL
#4 BEN'S IN LOVE
#5 CLAIRE GETS CAUGHT
#6 WHAT ZOEY SAW
#7 LUCAS GETS HURT
#8 AISHA GOES WILD
#9 ZOEY PLAYS GAMES
#10 NINA SHAPES UP
#11 BEN TAKES A CHANCE
#12 CLAIRE CAN'T LOSE
#13 DON'T TELL ZOEY
#14 AARON LETS GO
#15 WHO LOVES KATE?
#16 LARA GETS EVEN
#17 TWO-TIMING AISHA
#18 ZOEY SPEAKS OUT
#19 KATE FINDS LOVE
#20 NEVER TRUST LARA

Coming Soon

#21 TROUBLE WITH AARON

Avon Books are available at special quantity discounts for bulk purchases for sales promotions, premiums, fund raising or educational use. Special books, or book excerpts, can also be created to fit specific needs.

For details write or telephone the office of the Director of Special Markets, Avon Books, Inc., Dept. FP, 1350 Avenue of the Americas, New York, New York 10019, 1-800-238-0658.

Never trust Lara

KATHERINE APPLEGATE

AN AVON FLARE BOOK

AVON BOOKS, INC.
1350 Avenue of the Americas
New York, New York 10019

Copyright © 1997 by Daniel Weiss Associates, Inc.,
and Katherine Applegate
Published by arrangement with Daniel Weiss Associates, Inc.
Library of Congress Catalog Card Number: 99-94488
ISBN: 0-380-81309-2
www.avonbooks.com/chathamisland

First Avon Flare Printing: January 2000

AVON FLARE TRADEMARK REG. U.S. PAT. OFF. AND IN OTHER COUNTRIES, MARCA REGISTRADA, HECHO EN U.S.A.

Printed in the U.S.A.

WCD   10   9   8   7   6   5   4   3   2   1

For Michael

Never trust Lara

One

Zoey Passmore's eyes roved from the stove to the dishwasher to the juicer and finally lit on the fridge, where they studied the mess of family photos and outdated invitations. For a moment they lingered on a picture taken at graduation of Lucas Cabral holding her tightly in his arms, grinning straight into the camera. The camera had captured the precise quality of boyish candor that Zoey always admired in Lucas.

Or almost always. It was half an hour past the time Lucas had solemnly promised he'd call. Zoey's cowboy boots tapped against the stool. With a sigh of exasperation she leaped up and marched smartly past the hall phone to the mirror. She flung her dark blond hair back and surveyed herself in the glass. Yes, it was the same Zoey who only weeks before had been a mere high-school student. It was the same girl who'd been— ugh—voted Homecoming Queen runner-up. It was the same Zoey who Lucas had held in a loving grip in the photo on the fridge. Her deep blue eyes narrowed. She looked pretty good, staring fiercely at herself just now. The same Zoey.

"So why isn't that dork calling?" She swung from the mirror and faced the phone, glaring. *What am I thinking,* Zoey wondered. *That if I stare long enough at myself in the mirror, I'll make Lucas materialize?*

The sun was just peering over the clouds as Zoey slammed the door behind her and made her way up the little slope to the Cabrals'. Summer, always slow to arrive in Maine, was making a halting appearance. She felt the sun's comforting warmth on her bare arms and breathed a sigh of relief. Surely she was mistaken. She must have misunderstood Lucas when he said he would call to arrange a meeting place later that afternoon. It had been so long since they'd really hung out, especially alone. After his father's illness, Lucas had been obliged to work long hours on the fishing boat, but even Lucas's hard work and dedication wasn't enough to make up for the money lost from his father's absence. Lucas had had little time or energy left for anything when he got home from work. Zoey felt a pang of guilt as she reached the Cabrals' front door. Did she really have any right to complain or pester Lucas at a time like this?

Her question was answered momentarily. Before she had even knocked, the door of the house opened and Zoey found herself staring into the hard, stern face of Mr. Cabral.

"Lucas isn't here."

"Oh—oh, Mr. Cabral, I'm sorry. . . ." Zoey was flustered. Mr. Cabral was even gruffer than usual.

"He's out on the boat. And if you're thinking of waiting around for him to get back, I wouldn't. That kid's got a lot of work to do. You'd best find yourself another playmate, young lady."

Zoey swallowed. Mr. Cabral was always a bit short with her—sometimes, she imagined, because he didn't approve of the amount of energy Lucas gave to a girl instead of schoolwork or athletics—but this was

2

unusual. She backed down the stairs. She could feel her face growing hot.

"I'm sorry, I—I—I—I was just expecting, I mean . . ." She bit her lip. "It's just that he said he'd call and he hasn't and I was worried. He's very reliable. . . . Can you—"

Mr. Cabral cut her off. "Did you hear what I just said, young lady? The boy is working. He'll be working like this all summer, and so don't you go waiting around for any phone calls. And don't you be distracting him. The boy's got a duty to his family right now, and he doesn't need distractions." With that Mr. Cabral shut the door firmly in Zoey's face.

For a moment she stared straight ahead, as if she were still trying to register Mr. Cabral's words. Then her stomach dropped, and she could feel tears forming. She turned and ran back to the house, her face red with the sting of humiliation. Mr. Cabral barely listened to her! And he probably wouldn't have believed that Lucas was supposed to call even if he had listened.

Back at her house, it was all she could do to keep from sobbing as she dialed Nina Geiger's number.

"Nina?" Zoey was relieved that her friend picked up the phone and not Nina's sister, Claire, who Zoey didn't entirely trust.

"Zoey? Are you okay? You sound weird. What—did you catch a cold from too much fun on the treadmill?"

Zoey and Nina—at Nina's urging—had found summer work at a trendy gym in Weymouth. Zoey, needless to say, had outlasted Nina, who'd quit in a fit of frustration, disgusted with the too-perfect clientele showing off their sculpted bodies.

"Nina, this is serious. Nina . . ."

"Zo, are you crying?"

There was a sniffle at the end of the line.

"Zoey?"

"I'm okay, I'm okay . . . oh, Nina, it's just . . . it's just . . . oh, God, here I go."

Zoey felt the sobs welling up in her throat.

Nina was silent for a moment, waiting, then she said softly, "Zoey, this isn't like you. What happened? Don't worry—you can cry—I'm not gonna say something stupid. Hey, it's not that terrible PMS that's going around, is it?"

Zoey giggled through her tears. Nina could always be counted on to lift the gloomiest of moods with a joke.

"It's just that I'm at the end of my rope. Lucas— well, you know how he's been acting weird lately, kinda distant? Not coming to meet me at the gym a few days ago after he'd promised to? We were supposed to meet today, but he didn't call. I couldn't stand sitting there waiting, so I went up to the Cabrals' to see if he was home—"

"Zoey, what do you mean, you went up to his house? What did you think you would find, Lucas sitting there drumming his fingers on the table, going, 'Hmmm . . . I think I'll drive Zoey crazy today by not calling.'"

"Nina, listen. So it was stupid. But it was better than waiting around going crazy. Anyway, I get to Lucas's house and Mr. Cabral comes out and . . . and . . ."

"And what, Zoey?"

"Oh, I have to stop bawling. I don't even know why it upset me so much, except that Mr. Cabral always makes me nervous. I don't think he likes me, Nina."

"Zoey, c'mon, you're an in-laws' dream! Mr.

4

Cabral is just a little stuffy, that's all. I'm sure he likes you."

"He told me not to distract Lucas. He practically yelled. He called me 'young lady' and told me to find another playmate. I mean, it was awkward, to say the least."

Nina chuckled. "Young lady? You ought to be flattered. It sounds like a scene from a Katharine Hepburn movie."

Zoey had regained her calm sufficiently to glance out the kitchen window to the Cabrals' deck. She half expected to see Mr. Cabral standing with his arms crossed, watching to make sure Zoey wasn't frittering away Lucas's time on the telephone.

"Zoey, I'm sure Mr. Cabral likes you. I mean—I know he does—wasn't Lucas just saying something about that? He's just the kind of man who hates to be stuck home helpless while his family needs money. It sounds like he took it out on you. I'm sorry, Zo, I really am. Lucas really *just* said his dad loves you."

"He did? That's so nice. I'm glad you guys are actually able to have a conversation now. Wait, when *did* you have this conversation with Lucas?"

There was a slight pause on the other end of the line.

"Weeelll, today. Lucas was over here watching TV."

"What?" Zoey felt a confused shock run through her. What could Lucas possibly have been doing at Nina's—when he was supposed to be working or with her?

"Don't be mad, Zo. He just dropped by. I was kinda surprised. He talked about his dad and was all depressed—maybe he just doesn't want to hang out with you when he's depressed."

5

"Why didn't you mention this before? Nina—are you telling me that I was sitting around tortured by the sound of silence in my kitchen while Lucas lounged on your couch talking about how much his dad likes me? Is someone crazy here or is it just me?"

Zoey began angrily leafing through the newspaper, trying to keep her hands busy.

"Zoey, you were crying and upset! I didn't want to upset you more, but I was about to call you about it. Lucas is depressed, Zo. He loves you to death and he's embarrassed about himself. You should reach out and tell him you'd love to mope around the house with him. Boy, I'd be happy to hear those words out of Benjamin's mouth right now. . . ."

"Wait a minute!" Zoey's voice was suddenly lit with excitement. "I've got just the thing! Check out today's paper, Nina—look what's happening Friday night. . . ."

The surf washed over Benjamin Passmore as if he were just a piece of driftwood stuck in the sand. Lying on his back, staring up at the sun among the clouds and feeling the cool water rush over his stomach, Benjamin was in heaven.

Last week he'd been ready to give this up forever, just because of a little accident. Just because his doctors were overprotective and his eyes were still recovering from the surgery. But after a couple days of lying around inside, Benjamin had realized that what he wanted was a full recovery, and the only way to achieve that would be to build up his strength again. The bottom line was that his sight was back. And it would be a pathetic waste to not make use of it.

How could he have gone for days, months, years

without being free to throw himself at the waves, surfboard in hand?

It was disconcerting to realize how much his former, sightless life had been determined by calculation and caution. Twenty feet here. Thirty feet there. Now he could finally move with abandon, running without wondering what he would eventually run into. It was unbelievably, unbearably liberating. He loved the freedom of movement that surfing represented. He loved watching the experienced surfers attack each wave with cool deliberation, knowing that in a few months he, too, could attain that kind of ease and style. The world was simply mesmerizing and surfing was a perfect place to start living in the world.

A gull cried, and a shadow fell across his arm. He shivered. What time was it? How long had he been down at the beach? Ironically, gaining his sight had so overturned the old Benjamin system of sensing and measuring that he had gotten more disoriented and irresponsible, not less.

Nina was expecting him, and he would already be a few minutes late now. Benjamin dragged himself onto his feet and walked up the beach, looking wistfully back at the ocean and the few remaining surfers braving the chill. He hoisted his surfboard up and, for the sheer joy of it, began jogging in the direction of the Geigers' house.

When he knocked on the front door, Claire opened it. It was strange to think that once he had been in love with her. Now she seemed like a friendly stranger—almost.

"Well, well, look who's here. Mr. Surfer Dude himself, sporting a grin that won't go away. Nina's down in the TV room. Be my guest and go find her—she's been expecting you for, like, quite a while?" Claire winked.

"What happened, Claire—didn't get adored enough today? I'm so glad I can finally see that lovely sneer of yours." Benjamin smiled at Claire, ignoring her sultry wink.

And before he had even crossed the threshold into the TV room, Benjamin heard Nina's belligerent growl.

"I hope you got clobbered by some really big waves and have the stitches to show for it. Otherwise, you're one dead surfer."

Benjamin stared at the scene before him and smiled. Nina lay stretched out on the sofa, buried beneath a blanket and two empty bags of Doritos. On TV, Jenny Jones was mediating a catfight that had broken out between two guests. Nina nodded toward the TV.

"It's harsh. Women whose husbands have run off with the baby-sitter. That's one of them there now— the baby-sitter—with a ditched wife. You're only two hours late, Benjamin. See? One bag of Doritos for every hour."

"Two hours?" Benjamin's face dropped. "Wow— that means I was surfing for . . . five hours!" Aside from the fact that he'd upset Nina, Benjamin felt proud of himself. Time had gone by without him being aware of it in the slightest. He must have been really working hard.

"Surfing, huh. I was starting to think you'd run off with some cute surferette."

Benjamin paused. He knew Nina's sarcastic jokes disguised her real hurt, and the greater the hurt, the more the wisecracks. He realized guiltily that he'd not thought of her for the entire day he'd been surfing. Nina probably suspected this; in a way, it was worse to be forgotten altogether than briefly "ditched

8

for a surferette," as Nina so aptly put it. Benjamin considered how to best address her bruised ego.

"Nina—I know I'm acting weird, running off to the beach every day, showing up two hours late without even realizing it—but I can't tell you how exciting it is to be out there in the waves. I just want to catch up on everything I've missed. . . ."

"Like me, for example?" Nina interrupted, managing a halfhearted grin. But Benjamin ignored her.

"I'm sorry I lost track of time. I really am. Why don't you come surfing with me sometime? Then you'd understand it—"

"Thanks, Benjamin, I'd rather sit here with you drooling over the babes on *Baywatch* than the ones on the towel next to us."

Benjamin felt the last remnants of whatever remorse he'd been feeling over being late quickly melting. Why did Nina act as though he was such a mindless mimbo? "Nina, jeez. It's not about babes. Enough already on that."

Nina smiled ruefully and shook her head. "But you know, aside from all the kidding about girl watching, I don't like to surf. I don't even like beaches, for that matter, or any of the stuff you're supposed to have fun doing on them. Can't we just have one date, y'know, watching TV and reading aloud and goofing around indoors? You can't have changed that much. I mean, do you have to give up totally on your old life to have a new one?"

The truth was, as Benjamin settled onto the couch next to Nina with a sigh, that he was too anxious to experience the new things in life to care much about the old. Even the smell of the Geiger couch closing in on him as he lay back felt suffocating instead of familiar and reassuring. Of course Nina was as exciting to him as ever, even more: He loved watching the subtle expressions cross her face; he loved watching her mischievous eyes tell him things her voice never could. Just now, as she had stood up, stretching languidly, and rearranged herself on the couch at the opposite end so their legs were entwined beneath the blanket—he loved watching every muscle move. If only she could try to share his new pursuits, try to understand.

Nina began describing the saga going on on the talk show she'd watched. As he listened Benjamin realized how tired his muscles were from surfing. His thoughts drifted back to the blue sky framing the gray-green ocean surf. What were the colors on his surfboard, he wondered idly. . . .

"Benjamin. Benjamin." Nina was kicking him. "I can't believe this. I've been talking for practically the last half hour and you were asleep. Lucky your dad called or I'd have gone on all night. Wake up. He's on the phone." She thrust the receiver into his hand.

"Dad?" Benjamin felt groggy and disoriented.

"Benjamin?" His father sounded embarrassed. "I'm sorry if I'm—uh—disturbing anything. . . ."

"Oh, no, no," Benjamin said quickly, glancing at Nina. She looked away. "What is it? Why are you calling me here?"

"I thought you should know something. I got a call from the director of Serenity Hills today. It seems that Lara's run away."

"*What?*" Benjamin remembered the last time he'd seen his alcoholic half sister, drunk and passed out in his parents' living room.

"She's been gone since this morning. They're concerned for her safety, of course, as well as—frankly—ours. They know all about her breaking into

10

our house. She's been very resistant to treatment there, and they think she's probably going to run right out and get drunk. Once she's drunk—well, I'm worried, that's all."

"Oh, Dad." Benjamin slowly let out his breath. "This is awful."

"Do you think you could possibly take over my shift at the restaurant?" his father continued. "I'd like to take the car out and look for her. I know it's silly. But I can't just sit around waiting."

Benjamin hung up the phone slowly. Nina's irritation had given way to concern, and she stared at him wide-eyed.

"What is it? What happened?"

Benjamin shook his head.

"Lara's run away. She's totally out of control, and no one has a clue as to her whereabouts. Dad wants me to spot him at Passmores'." Benjamin managed an ironic smile, but he couldn't suppress the sense of dread he felt starting in his stomach.

TWO

Claire Geiger sat brushing her long, silky black hair. "I am not going to blow this," she muttered to herself. *I owe it to Aaron and my father.* She hesitated. *And Sarah, yes, I owe it to her, too, after everything I've done to make life with my dad miserable for her . . . but most of all I owe it to myself. Because I want Aaron. And it's my fault I've almost made that impossible.* She couldn't forget the faces of her father and Sarah Mendel when they'd come home early from the theater and found her on the couch with Aaron, passionately making out. He'd had one arm around her and one hand holding her chin as he pressed his lips against hers. She could remember now the slightly damp feel of his chest on hers, damp from the sweat of both their excitement. Her father had said that now, days later, he was finally calm enough to discuss the situation rationally. And as Claire prepared to go downstairs and face him and Sarah in what would be their first family "meeting" about the "Aaron and Claire" problem, a chill raced down her back.

Then it had been exciting, sure—until she looked up and saw her father standing on the threshold of the living-room door, car keys still in hand, staring at her and Aaron in horror; Sarah bustling in behind him, her usual inane chatter cut short by the astonishing sight of her son on top of her new stepdaughter.

If only she and Aaron had swallowed their pride and told their parents! Claire yanked at her hair savagely. She hated the fact that she had lost control of the situation. Instead of showing Burke and Sarah that she was a mature woman who could take responsibility for her choices, she had looked like an embarrassed, sneaky high-school girl—someone like Lara. Her father might find her occasionally manipulative and sometimes cruel, but he had always respected her maturity. It was Nina who might lie on a rebellious whim, or run away, or get in trouble by acting irresponsibly. But Claire, well, Claire was supposed to be the mature one of the two Geiger sisters. Claire was the scientist going to MIT, the one who'd inherited the banker genes in the family. And now her father sat waiting for her downstairs, more disappointed in her than he'd ever been.

She looked hard at herself in the mirror. Was it just her father's disappointment that weighed on her? She pursed her lips pensively. Or was it also the humiliation of her father's newly justified involvement in her love life?

"Claire?" Aaron called up the stairs.

It was now or never. She took one last look in the mirror. It was hardly the time to be vain, but seeing her pale, coldly elegant reflection gave her a quick rush of calm, as it always did.

"Claire?" Aaron tapped on her door, then opened it, breathless from running up the stairs. "Show's on. Are you ready?" He gave her a wry, conspiratorial smile. "Should I carry you down the stairs and into the dining room, Rhett Butler style? Or maybe that might not give the right impression?"

"Smart-ass. It might be wiser to enter the dining room crawling on our hands and knees."

Aaron smirked faintly and then gestured at the stairs. "Whichever way we do it, I suggest we do it now, or they'll think we got overcome with lust and forgot about them."

Claire stood up straight and took a deep breath. "I'll go first," she murmured, and slipped quickly past Aaron. She could hear her father's voice as she went down the stairs. How would he handle the "discussion" (as he put it)? Burke was generally a sensible, mild man, but he could be unpredictable. Claire had seen him blow up at clients who'd reneged on their loan contracts, and it wasn't a sight she wished to relive. Now as she rounded the corner she could hear an edge of defensiveness in his tone.

"Look, she's my daughter; I ought to know, Sarah. I think you're being too judgmental. After all—"

"Hi, guys," Claire interrupted. "Sorry I'm a little late. I was napping upstairs." She gave both of them a wide, friendly grin.

Her father, who had been leaning toward Sarah, sat back abruptly in his chair.

"Claire, darling. I, uh—here, sit down and have some snacks." He gestured at the bowl of chips on the table. Claire could tell from her father's slightly sweaty brow that he was flustered. Sarah, on Claire's entrance, had immediately switched composures from a frown to her usual simper.

Mr. Geiger cleared his throat and adjusted his shirt

as Aaron walked in and sat down. *So that's it,* Claire mused. *Dad's going to play bad cop while Sarah pretends to be nice and understanding.* She felt her blood start to race. Thank goodness Nina was out. She would have loved this scene, particularly if Claire lost her self-control. *But I am not going to lose my temper,* Claire reminded herself firmly.

Sarah broke the awkward silence. "We don't need to remind the two of you how disappointed we are by your dishonesty."

Claire groaned inwardly. She hated it when Sarah or her father said "we," as if getting married allowed them to operate now as one parental unit. How dare Sarah think she had any right to punish Claire or make decisions for her?

"We've gone over all that a million times. But what I don't think I've impressed on you kids enough is how worried we are"—Sarah hesitated, as if she could read Claire's mind—"well, let me speak for myself here—how worried I am about your relationship. I just think that it's unhealthy, to say the very least, and that it could potentially create a huge rift in a family we're just beginning to make." She paused, Claire thought, for dramatic effect: "I'm just very torn up about this. Really." She turned her shining, sympathetic eyes toward Aaron for recognition. Claire, turning also, noticed with annoyance that Aaron looked totally relaxed, as if the four of them were discussing their next family vacation. *Doesn't he understand that the future of our relationship is at stake?* she wondered.

"And Claire." Sarah turned back to look at Claire. She smiled. "You're an extraordinary girl, the kind of girl I'd be thrilled to have my son dating . . . under any other circumstances. I don't want you to take this personally, I really don't. . . ."

Claire felt her heart beat faster. She couldn't stand Sarah's phony act. She tried to meet Aaron's eyes, but he was looking at his mother.

"Just what are you trying to say, Sarah?" Claire heard her own voice as if it were someone else's.

Mr. Geiger hurriedly intervened. "What we're trying to tell both of you is that we think you need to see other people. We want you to break off your involvement, for the time being, and think more about the ramifications of your actions in terms of the entire family. We want you to look around and, well, play the field for a while. Claire—do you understand?" Mr. Geiger spoke sharply to his daughter, who stared sullenly at the table.

There was a silence. Aaron took a breath and began to speak, but it was too late. Claire couldn't stifle her resentment any longer. Ignoring Aaron, she snapped, "Oh, yeah, right, Dad. Like you can tell me who to go out with. Could I have told you not to go out with that stupid bitch?" She gestured at Sarah. "She's hardly Mom, Dad. And now I'm stuck with her for the rest of my life!"

Oh, no, Claire thought the instant the words were out of her mouth. This wasn't the way it was supposed to go. Her insides twisted. *Now I've called my boyfriend's mother and my father's wife a bitch!* But along with her agony she felt also relief. She had wanted to say it for a long, long time now.

Mr. Geiger swore under his breath. "Claire, don't you ever speak about my wife like that again!" His voice was cold and deadly quiet. "Sarah—I apologize for my daughter. She's obviously venting issues

16

about her mother's death. I should have anticipated more of this. Please, darling . . ."

But it was too late. Tears streamed down Sarah's face. With a look of pained bewilderment she ran from the room.

Claire forced herself to look at Aaron. But he wouldn't meet her eyes. He seemed to be staring straight ahead in shock, his eyes unfocused and glassy.

What was he thinking? Claire couldn't stand it another second. "Aaron? I'm so, so—"

At the sound of her words Aaron seemed to snap back into reality. He stumbled out of his chair, muttering something about going to comfort his mother.

The spaces left by the two Mendels were unbearably empty.

Claire turned to her father. He sat motionless, with his head in his hands.

"No one can ever replace your mother, Claire. I know that."

Claire felt her heart lurch. Was her father crying? "Dad—Dad—I'm sorry," she stammered.

When he spoke again, it was with surprising gentleness. "You're going to have to work hard to build trust back with Sarah, Claire. You've done a lot of damage in a very short time." He looked hard into his daughter's eyes. "I don't envy you what you must be feeling."

Claire said nothing. A lump had risen in her throat, preventing her from speaking another word. She wanted to tell her father that it wasn't Sarah—that Sarah had merely been a scapegoat. But she knew that he knew.

"All right. In a little while I think you should go

talk to Sarah. In the meantime—Claire, I don't think you should be seeing Aaron. I have a colleague at the bank who has a son your age. Why don't you ask him out Friday night?"

Claire could only nod through her tears.

"That'll be three-fifty." The woman behind the counter of the art supply store waited patiently. Lara McAvoy handed her a five and smiled brightly.

"Would you know when the ferry leaves for Chatham Island, by any chance?"

The woman seemed happy to oblige her new customer, and Lara left the store beaming.

It had worked! If the cashier at the art supply store she frequented hadn't recognized her, Zoey never would. Lara glanced at her reflection in the shop window. It was odd to see the long brown curly wig where she expected to find her own short blond hair. It made her look, well, older. Safer. The kind of girl you would expect to find boarding a ferry for Chatham Island. The kind of sensible girl who might be teaching sailing lessons or tutoring disadvantaged youth for the summer.

Lara giggled out loud. Not the kind of girl who had just escaped from a rehab clinic.

The twelve-thirty P.M. ferry was preparing to depart when Lara raced up the gangway. For the first time since she'd met her real father, she felt happy to be on the ferry. For the first time she took real pleasure in the brisk ocean breeze and the taste of salt in her mouth. The stench of liquor on her breath had prevented her from ever noticing the fresh, salty air before. She squinted at the outline of Chatham Island in the distance. *Little do they know who they're dealing with,* she thought. She bristled with rage as she ran through the events of the past weeks in her mind. Her father, the one who hadn't even raised her— who'd run off to raise two other perfect little brats— had sent her, against her will, to a rehab clinic. And what a jail it was. Now, out here in the open sea, the meaning of her escape sank in.

I'm a genius, Lara congratulated herself giddily. She felt caressed by the wonderful June breeze, exalted by the sense of possibility. Why had that stupid priss Zoey ever even bothered her? Lara knew what Zoey was—a boring little sorority girl who would end up writing articles about lost pets for a small-town newspaper. Why, Zoey could never begin to understand Lara's paintings or Lara's knowledge of people. Still, it was Zoey who Lara hated the most of all of them. Zoey was Lara's nemesis: From the minute they'd met, Lara was sure Zoey had had it in for her.

It was all Zoey's fault.

But Lara felt sure she could exact retribution. There had been a moment at Serenity Hills when the churning in her stomach and the racing in her head had stopped. Thinking back, she couldn't put her finger on the exact moment—it might have been in the midst of one of those stupid "support group" sessions, after one of her humiliating calls to Jake. Or it might have been the morning she woke up from a recurring nightmare (she dreamed always that she was dying of thirst) and found she didn't need a drink. Whenever it was, it stood out because her rage no longer felt helpless. Instead she felt calm and self-assured.

Only one thing was left to be done. And that was figuring out *what* to do. Lara grinned and tossed her wig, pretending she was Farah Fawcett in *Charlie's*

Angels. The ferry was arriving, and she shivered with excitement. She imagined Jake watching her walk glamorously down the gangway, wondering who the "new girl" was and why she looked oddly familiar. Jake loved James Bond, didn't he?

Lara glanced at her watch. She had to hurry if she was going to catch Zoey on her way to work. Her plan thus far was this: Follow Zoey to work and, if necessary, eat at the restaurant. It seemed like the best place to start. The Passmores' restaurant was the hub of all social activity on the island. Unless you counted the circle at the center of North Harbor—but it was too windy a day for people to hang out there, and besides, Zoey was the real social hub of North Island, and she would be at work. What exactly Lara would gain from spying on Zoey, she wasn't sure, but where else could she start? She couldn't exactly walk into the Passmore household. *Hi, everybody, it's me, Lara—I broke out of the jail you dumped me in and I'm back for revenge. By the way, is Zoey in?*

Exiting the ferry, Lara felt her stomach tighten. Everything was the same: the quaint boats in the harbor, the cobblestoned streets, the cute little white-washed houses. It all made her sick. And Jake was here somewhere, too. Would he be the same—the same A.A.-abiding drip under the spell of a conniving Kate?

She quickened her steps, moving purposefully down Dock Street to where it intersected with South Street. She knew it would only be minutes before Zoey appeared. Unless she was late. *Unlikely,* Lara scoffed. *We're talking about Zoey Passmore, Miss Priss—who wouldn't even be late to a job she couldn't get fired from.* Lara paused, her eyes searching for a spot where she wouldn't be noticed by Zoey's curious, interested gaze.

Her eyes ran along the white picket fence lining the yard of the corner cottage. Tulips and daffodils burst through slots of the fence in an exuberant, disorderly fashion. The gate was shut firmly, and the front window shades were drawn. If it weren't for the chaotic blooming of the spring flowers, the cottage would seem deserted.

Footsteps echoed down South Street, approaching at a fast clip. Lara panicked. Without thinking, she jumped the picket fence and bent down among the flowers. *If Zoey notices me, she'll think I'm a landscaper.* Lara began digging industriously away at the dirt beneath the flowers. *No one will notice if a few flowers are missing,* she thought, excitedly bringing up a handful of roots and dirt. Out of the corner of her eye she peered at the street.

It was Zoey, all right. Practically skipping, she looked so cheerful. Lara wanted to puke. Zoey's hair was shining blond in the sun, and her face looked expectant. Lara narrowed her eyes. Something was up. Zoey never hid anything on her face; she couldn't if she tried. Zoey looked as if she were bursting with news. What could it be? Lara's eyes followed her all the way down the street.

Zoey

Ever since I was a little girl, I've loved carnivals. I remember Mom and Dad taking me to a fair in Boston that had an old-fashioned carousel. I wanted to ride each of the brightly painted, carved animals, so I stayed on the carousel for almost the entire day. My favorite was the swan. I pretended I was a gypsy traveling with the carnival and that at night I would sneak out to the carousel and ride the swan, who became real at my touch. Mom tells me I cried and had to be pulled from the swan after the carousel stopped.

Maybe it's childish, but

there's a big carnival in
Weymouth this summer and
I'm just as excited about
it now as I would have
been then. Not that any of
the things I've been
excited about lately have
really been turning out
the way I expected. I
mean, I was so excited
about graduating, and the
summer, and then... then
what?

I guess I was looking
forward to spending time
with Lucas before I go
away to California in the
fall. Well, Lucas is
depressed. He has to work
all summer when it's the
last summer we have
together. It's not his
fault he has to work so
hard. I shouldn't feel
rejected. Frustrated, lonely,
desperately helpless, okay—

I mean, there's not really anything I can do about the situation. But I shouldn't feel rejected. So why do I? Because Lucas is either acting depressed or blowing me off altogether. Sometimes I don't understand him. Why won't he at least talk to me about what he's feeling?

I wish I could get Lucas to come to the carnival with me. I'm sure it would cheer him up. And I couldn't think of a more romantic setting. Maybe for one night we could just forget everything that's happened—his dad's illness, my going away to school in the fall. Maybe for one night we could just be kids again.

Three

"Excuse me, waitress . . ." Aisha Gray giggled, gesturing at Zoey, who was carrying an armful of ketchup bottles into the kitchen. "But didn't you forget my coffee?"

Zoey rolled her eyes.

"Excuse me, Miss Gray," Zoey mimicked, "but aren't you being a little pushy for a nice regular like you? Have you, like, *noticed* that the restaurant is practically full and I'm still refilling the ketchup? Not to mention that I worked all morning at the health club and I'm already exhausted. Bother me any more and you'll get coffee on your French toast instead of maple syrup."

"Well." Aisha affected a shocked, hurt look. "What a sassy waitress I have."

She watched Zoey dash madly back and forth from the kitchen. Zoey was as fast and efficient a waitress as she was a swimmer. She never wasted a motion but still smiled and chatted with the customers. It was fun to watch her work.

Fun to watch when you wanted to distract yourself from other things, Aisha thought, disgusted with herself. Why didn't she confront Christopher and make him tell her why he didn't want Aisha to spend time with his sister? She shook her head. Either she was the biggest sucker in the world or she just didn't understand the world—and that was unbearable for logical, cool Aisha Gray.

Why won't the restaurant quiet down so I can talk to Zoey? Aisha looked around the room in dismay. Who were all these people, anyway? *Since when does the entire town of North Harbor try and squeeze into the Passmores' restaurant?* She noticed that Benjamin was back in the kitchen. Only now, in the weeks since he'd recovered his sight, had he begun to help out in the family restaurant. Aisha's eyes fell on a girl hunched over in the corner by herself. She looked vaguely familiar. Aisha wondered if she went to Weymouth High. But maybe she was a bit older. It was hard to tell what her face looked like beneath all her hair.

Aisha looked out the window at Dock Street, lost in her own internal argument. What were her options, anyway?

1. *Find Kendra alone and demand to know what her story was;*
2. *Sneak over to Christopher's house and eavesdrop on the two of them;*
3. *Refuse to speak to or see Christopher until he told her the truth;*
4. *Stop making dumb lists like this and respect Christopher's wishes. As her mom liked to say, it would all come out in the wash eventually.*

Aisha smiled at the thought of herself refusing to speak to or see Christopher until he told her more about his sister. That would last a whole ten minutes.

"Eesh?"

It was Zoey, calling her from the next table. She was wiping the table with a damp rag.

"I'm so glad you came to the restaurant. Wait till I tell you what's going on. . . ."

"Well—are you going to tell me or what?"

Zoey moved away from the table.

"In a sec—wait till the place has thinned out so I can really talk to you. I've got to get these orders served." And she raced off to the kitchen without a backward glance.

When Zoey stepped away from the table next to her, Aisha saw the strange girl in the corner suddenly look up at them, as if she were struck by something they had said. Aisha noticed it because their eyes naturally met, but before Aisha had a chance to smile, the girl looked away quickly. *That's odd,* Aisha mused. But why? Anyone who overheard a tantalizing conversation like theirs might look up. *Am I going crazy, suspicious of every girl on Chatham Island who I don't know well?* She shook her head. *I am not going to let this get to me,* she told herself severely.

In a few minutes the customers had all been served, and Zoey came to stand next to Aisha's table.

"Okay . . . are you ready?" Her blue eyes widened. "I'm dying of anticipation. . . ."

"Eesh—Lara's escaped from that asylum, or wherever it was they were keeping her. Dad's out looking for her now."

"You're kidding. Your parents must be freaking out." Aisha patted Zoey sympathetically on the arm. "How are you holding up?"

"I'm not going to let her get me down," Zoey answered. "There's too much going on in my life right now. And I just hope I don't run into her in a dark alley or anything."

"That would certainly be an adventure," Aisha answered wryly. Was it just her imagination or was the girl with the hair leaning forward, listening to their conversation?

"Speaking of adventure," Zoey said, "a huge carnival's coming to the Weymouth on Friday. I think we should all go together. It's what we all need right now. Whaddya say?"

"A carnival? Really? Like a Ferris wheel and fortune-tellers and roller coaster kind of carnival? Or just farmers with prize pigs?"

"Like, no pigs. A zillion roller coasters."

Aisha gave Zoey a wide, phony grin. "Zoey— that's fantastic!" she said. "I can't wait to smooch Christopher on the Ferris wheel."

Zoey shook her head, smiling. "Sorry, Eesh. Lucas and I called it first." She paused, then spoke more conspiratorially. "Lucas has been really depressed about working so hard and stuff. I think he's afraid he's going to turn into his father and be trapped on Chatham Island or something. The carnival will be—"

"Miss?" A customer waved at Zoey, gesturing for the check. Zoey went to his table, talking over her shoulder at Aisha.

"Anyway, we'll all have a blast. Do you think Christopher will bring, uh . . ."

"The mystery sister?" Aisha smoothly finished the sentence. "How could he not? She's like his shadow. Even though he won't let me speak one word to her. She's probably not his sister at all. Or maybe she is his sister, and they're both aliens, and she's just checking in from her home planet or something."

"Just call Christopher and make sure he can go, okay? I'll distract Kendra and give her plenty of information about life on earth while you guys ride the Ferris wheel alone. And help me think of how to cheer Lucas up . . . I'll be right back." Zoey ran off to the kitchen.

Aisha felt someone watching her. She looked up only to find the girl in the corner looking down at her drink. *But I know she was watching me,* Aisha thought. *Why is she watching me? Does she think she knows me? Does she somehow tie in with Kendra—or Christopher?*

When Zoey returned, Aisha listened to her complain about Lucas until her paranoia got the better of her.

"Zoey, I'm sorry to interrupt . . . but do you know that girl?" She pointed to the corner. Zoey turned, her eyes following Aisha's finger. No one was there.

"What girl?"

Aisha stuttered. "Th-Th-The one that was just there, you know, five minutes ago. She's been looking at me all this time. Did you notice anything about her?"

"Aisha, it's been so busy, and besides, I've been thinking so much about the carnival, I wasn't looking at any of my customers. I'm sorry . . . are you sure—"

"Oh, never mind. It was nothing." Aisha shook her head.

"She must have left in a hurry," said Zoey. She walked over to the table and counted up the money left on the counter.

"And she didn't leave a tip."

Leaving the Passmores' restaurant, Lara was so excited, she forgot she was in disguise and supposed to act inconspicuous.

Now I know where I can find them all Friday night . . . and I might even have an idea about what to do to them. . . .

She gave a passing old lady a big, huge grin.

"Hello, dearie. Aren't you sweet." The old lady smiled back.

Yup, Lara said to herself. *Sweet might not quite be the word, but . . .*

She walked briskly down to the pay phone bank at the dock. Now that she'd accomplished plan A, getting a plan (well, okay, it wasn't quite done yet—she had to make a few essential inquiries at the Weymouth wharf), now it was time for plan B.

She dropped a quarter into the pay phone slot and dialed a number. She waited, checking her reflection a few times as she twirled her long, tawny hair around the tip of one finger.

"Hello?"

It was Mrs. Passmore.

Lara took a deep breath. When she asked for Mr. Passmore, her voice came out lower, without its usual alcohol-slurred intonation. Instead it sounded pleasant and self-possessed.

"May I speak to Jeff?" She didn't want to bother revealing herself to Mrs. Passmore. Not just yet. Anyway, Mr. Passmore would surely tell her about the conversation.

"Hello?" Mr. Passmore got on the line.

"Dad?"

"Lara?" He sounded surprised. "Is that you? My God, where are you? I went out looking for you. I've been so worried—Lara—you—"

"Dad, I know I did a terrible thing, running away from Serenity Hills." Lara was surprised at how sincere she sounded. *I'm pretty good at this,* she thought.

30

"Lara, I've been furious. What are you doing? Why did you run away?" His voice sounded tense and clipped. Lara could tell she wasn't getting to him yet.

"Dad, I had to leave." She tried to sound remorseful and upset. "It did wonders for me, it really did, and I'm so glad you sent me there. I owe it all to you. But I couldn't stay, not after I'd kicked it. You know, I want to do the rest of it myself. I want to prove to myself and to you and to everyone . . ."

"Lara—are you saying you've stopped drinking? You haven't had a drink since you left Serenity Hills?"

"Do I sound drunk?"

"Nooo . . ." His voice was doubtful.

"I've stopped drinking. I'm not going to have another drink. I'm going to start going to A.A. meetings with Jake. If I have to, I'll go every day."

"A.A. meetings?"

"Dad, I know you're stunned. I've made a decision to stop screwing up my life. Just like you said. And I'm going to pay you back all the money I owe you. All of it. The money I stole from the restaurant and whatever amount it was that I consumed in liquor."

There was a pause. Lara bit at her cuticles anxiously.

"Uh, Dad?"

"Yes, Lara. I'm here. I'm just trying to understand all this. It's quite a surprise, you know. I hardly expected you to call up and apologize. Let's see—you're telling me you left Serenity Hills so you could recover on your own, going to A.A. meetings with Jake?"

"Yes." She made her voice quaver with emotion.

"And how do you plan to pay me back? I'm not giving you a job at the restaurant."

"I'll find a job. I'm job hunting right now, and I'll call you the moment I know where I'll be working. I want you to trust me, Dad."

"Hmmm." Jeff Passmore sounded puzzled, but the wariness in his voice lifted. "Lara, I've never heard you sound this way before. I have to admit, this is all very encouraging. I had about thrown in—well—er, you know. . . ."

"I know, Dad." Lara's voice softened. *You bet you had almost thrown in the towel, you bastard.*

"I know. I know how badly I've behaved." *I can't believe I'm kissing butt this much.*

"Lara, I'm proud of you. Will you call as soon as you've figured out what you're doing?"

I already know what I'm doing.

"Of course I will."

"Good-bye, Lara. Good luck."

"Good-bye, Dad. And Dad? Please give my love to Benjamin and Zoey. . . ."

Four

Jake escorted a greenish Kate out of a bumper car, his favorite carnival ride.

"I think I could sue you for, like, bodily harm. I swear I have whiplash." Kate whimpered, rubbing her neck. It was Friday night, and all the island kids had broken up into couples. Kate thoughtfully suggested they start with Jake's favorite ride. She was regretting this. Jake nuzzled her in apology.

"Kate, I can't help it if I'm a big macho football player and you're a thin, sexy supermodel. Who do you think's gonna get smushed?"

"Okay, enough with the supermodel bit. Just get me out of here before some seven-year-old knocks me over in their bumper car. Jake, those bumper cars were worse than New York City taxis, and I thought that was something I'd never be able to say."

"Oh, honey, I'm terrible. I promise we'll go on your favorite ride, like, a hundred times."

"Ride? Who said my favorite carnival activity is a ride?" Kate quipped. She looked up at Jake and smiled. "Can you guess what I like best? I'll give you a hint: Think weird visual perspectives. Think cameras. Think artsy photography girls."

Kate's parents had taken her to Coney Island

when she was a child, and while fascinated by everything, she'd lingered for hours in front of the House of Mirrors and in later years found herself returning again and again. The mirrors did to her what she hoped to do to others with her camera: transform them by showing an aspect of themselves they hadn't known existed. Now, as she led a puzzled Jake past the Moonwalk, she was embarrassed to notice butterflies in her stomach. And they weren't from the bumper cars. *I'm worried Jake will think the House of Mirrors is stupid,* she realized. *Why am I always afraid of revealing myself?*

"The shooting range?" Jake guessed, scratching his head. Kate burst out laughing.

"You know, artsy photography girls, shooting cameras, guns, hey—I don't know. . . ." He gave her a playful grin.

Kate stopped. "Nope. Here we are."

"The House of Mirrors? Oh, the funny mirrors—I should have known! That's cool, Kate."

Kate breathed a sigh of relief. Jake was always so . . . kind.

Inside the fun house Jake howled with laughter at the sight of his enormously fat reflection. "I'd make a killer quarterback, huh?"

"Hey, Jake, wait a minute—look in the mirror above us." Kate pointed over their heads. The top of the mirror reflected a snatch of the crowd milling outside the fun house.

"Isn't that Claire? With—who's that weird guy?"

Jake squinted up at the mirror. "I'll be darned—I think you're right—Claire with a supernerdy guy? Wow—this is even crazier than seeing myself look like a six-hundred-pound sumo wrestler!"

Claire stood with her hand on her hips, trying to

disappear into the crowd. *I hope none of my friends see me with this dope,* she thought. The night had thus far been a disaster. Before he arrived to pick her up, Claire had hoped to spend the evening with a pleasant, inoffensive guy who wouldn't drool over her breasts too excessively. It was bad enough that she had to spend a Friday night away from Aaron. She didn't want to even *think* about how much fun they would have had at the carnival.

But from the moment Steven had offered her his hand in greeting she had known he was going to get on her nerves. Her first thought was that he was straight out of a late-night television infomercial for get-rich-quick tapes. He was a nerd who made himself more ridiculous by trying too hard *not* to be a nerd. Claire pegged him as one of those guys who compensated for his insecurity around women by putting on a supersmooth routine. He talked incessantly about his glorious ambitions, all the while leering at her body. But the worst of it, Claire thought bitterly, was that she was forced to remain civil to him for the sake of her father. Steven's father was one of Burke's best employees, and he relied on him heavily.

Now here she was at the carnival, fighting to keep her ire under control while he prattled on about his Model United Nations activities and golf.

"Do you think they have putt-putt? Check it out— my average last summer was five hundred par. My dad even let me go to some tournaments in Florida. To watch, of course, heh, heh." He checked her face to see if she appreciated the joke.

Oh, how big of you. Claire groaned. *You can even afford to be self-deprecating.* She plastered a smile on her face. At least maybe she could have some fun with him—at his expense.

"So is miniature golf your favorite thing to do at a carnival?" She affected a syrupy sweet tone.

He was pleased to have her full attention. "My favorite thing to do? . . . Hmmm. I know it's weird, but it probably is—I mean, I know the rides are really cool and all, but I just love golf, you know—can't beat golf for a great time."

Golf. She could barely suppress giggles. What a dullard. She felt sorry for the poor girl who would end up with Steven, twiddling her thumbs while he shot golf balls through windmills.

"What's your favorite ride, Claire?"

Claire was taken aback. At last he'd asked *her* something. She figured his nervous rambling precluded such basic conversational etiquette. Carefully ironing out the irritation in her voice, she told him— looking forward to his reaction.

"Are you for real? No way . . ."

That was the usual response when Claire told people how much she enjoyed target practice. Although she'd never actually been to a rifle range, she'd spent countless afternoons in arcades or at carnival booths perfecting her shot.

"It's the kind of person I am," she'd once explained on-line to Sean. For a short time she'd actually imagined that she and Sean could be more than just friends, but that had been before she'd met him and realized that she wasn't physically attracted to him. "I like control. I like to have a target, I like to strategize—mathematically or scientifically— about how to reach that target, and then I like to reach it. Shooting is like a cruder version of my passion for weather because weather patterns are the ultimate uncontrollable target." Sean, she reflected, had been the only person who had really understood it without simply thinking she was a competitive bitch.

"Hey, can I see you take a shot? Maybe you could win me a stuffed pink bunny." Steven chortled at his own joke.

Claire tossed her hair, resenting the implicit reference to their "date."

"You look like the kinda guy who needs a pink bunny. Why not?" She smiled at him nastily.

Steven's face went blank, and then he looked away. For the first time that evening there was silence as they walked to the shooting arcades.

Serves him right, Claire fumed. She wondered what Aaron was doing and if he felt even a twinge of jealousy.

"Hey, look at that ride—pretty wild, huh?" Steven pointed across the way to a fake pirate ship that went completely upside down on its axis, making a full circle faster and faster. People were screaming so loud, Claire could have sworn they were sitting next to her. She nodded. "Once my sister and I went on that when we were little. My dad dared us, and my sister threw up. She hates those kinds of rides now."

Claire's eyes widened. "Speaking of the devil," she muttered, "that couldn't be Nina, could it, in line for the Pirate Ship?"

"I'm sorry?" Steven asked politely.

Claire halted and squinted at the line of people waiting to go on the ride. "My sister—the one I was just talking about—this is such a crazy coincidence— I think that's her!" She pointed at a figure leaning on the rail, looking dejectedly at the ship as it swung wildly past her.

"She's not in line for the ride. She seems to be waiting for someone to get off it."

"Yes, Steven, you're right." *She's waiting for Ben-*

jamin, of course. It occurred to Claire in a flash that Nina was spending the evening watching Benjamin enjoy rides she hated. A wave of sympathy washed over Claire, and she wanted to reach out to her forlorn sister to comfort her.

"That's your sister? Gee, I guess I got lucky to be out with you, didn't I?" Steven remarked crassly.

"Shut up." Claire's mouth set in a cold line. "Do you want to shoot some guns or what?" She marched off in the direction of the arcade.

Look at all these babes. Nina sighed. She felt awkward and obtrusive standing at the railing of the Pirate Ship—the fourth railing at which she'd stood just in the last hour. *Why did I think this dumb outfit would make me feel better?* Nina had thought her conception of an anticarnival outfit hilarious at the time. Now the dumpy brown sweater and her father's pin-striped work pants just made her feel stupid. And butt ugly. And Benjamin had hardly appreciated the gesture. "Why are those pants so big? And maybe you should wear colors tonight, Nina, so you don't disappear into the night and get lost from me," he'd said.

And it was exactly what she now wanted to do. How could she be so conscious of people *not* looking at her, she wondered. All night she'd stood watching guys checking girls out in the lines or making eyes as they walked past one another, or worse, she'd watched happy couples disembark hand in hand, cheeks flushed, oblivious to her even as they were knocking past her at the exit. She'd felt smaller and smaller, shrinking into the night as it got brighter with lights and bigger with laughter.

This sucks. She wondered what would happen if

she slipped away and ran home before Benjamin got off the ride. Would he really care? *I'm just ruining what would otherwise be a brilliant night for him,* she thought glumly. For the first few rides Benjamin had shouted and waved at her. But the gesture had soon become forced, and Nina barely bothered to look up at him now. *What kills me,* she reflected, *is that he understands why I don't like carnivals—he really understands—having spent so much of his own life as an outsider.*

"It's that feeling," she'd explained, "of being coerced into having fun. I start immediately *not* having fun. Carnivals are like keg parties, or parades, or New Year's Eve—people look at you like you're the biggest loser if you're not having the best night of your life. It's like they're not happy unless you're doing cartwheels down the street."

Benjamin had laughed and hugged her and said he *totally* understood and—ta-da—here she was, leaning on the railing of the Pirate Ship, landing site of her childhood stomach contents, circa 1989.

She sighed and turned to watch the Ferris wheel. *That's where I belong—along with all the other old ladies.* But as if to spite her, she spotted Aisha and Christopher snuggled up in one of the cars. They had seen her and were waving excitedly. Christopher grabbed Aisha and kissed her, and then they both looked at Nina and broke into peals of laughter.

Nina raised a limp hand and waved slowly back. *They can't see my tears from so high up,* she reassured herself.

Five

"Nina looks so cute in that outfit—I swear she's wearing her dad's pants!" Aisha had her head on Christopher's shoulder. It was the third time in a row they'd gone on the Ferris wheel, Aisha's favorite ride. The Ferris wheel made her think of porch swings and pink lemonade on soft summer nights. She liked the slow, calm creaking of the cars and the quiet excitement you felt when you reached the top and saw the entire raucous carnival below. The Ferris wheel had a sentimental, romantic effect on her; she appreciated its history and its tradition. She couldn't imagine anything better than sitting snuggled up next to Christopher, with the whole summer stretched before them.

"Christopher?"

"Mmmm?" He stroked her cheek.

"When we get to the top again—wouldn't it be a nice time to tell me what's going on with Kendra?"

"Nice try, babe. Look, Kendra is my sister, and I love her, but she's my past. I don't see why my past has to mix with my future." Christopher smiled and held Aisha closer.

"Oh." Aisha's voice was annoyed. She sighed. "Okay. So I'll just never get a chance to talk to my fiancé's sister. That makes perfect sense."

Christopher laughed. "You are a persistent girl, even on the Ferris wheel. That's why I love you. By the way, Aisha, are we ever getting off this love nest? 'Cuz I got a hankering for the roller coaster. The Big Dipper."

"Christopher, I don't think of you as a roller-coaster man!" Aisha drew back and gave him a quizzical look. "You're not the crazy, manic-depressive type."

"Who said you had to be manic-depressive to like the roller coaster? Aisha, I'm a businessman. Business—true business—is just like a roller coaster. You know, you inch slowly up to the top, cautious, working hard, sweating hard—and then, just at the right moment, you take a deep breath and you let 'em roll! You risk everything you have because you've got to. Then you win big, and you hunker down again. Stay low. Wait until another moment arises. That's the roller coaster."

"Well. I know who to turn to if I write my Ph.D. dissertation on metaphors of success in America. Gee, Christopher, I should have known."

They were both still laughing as they finally climbed out of the car. Aisha told Christopher to wait while she ran to the bathroom.

In the bathroom Aisha lingered in front of the mirror, redoing the little makeup she'd put on for the occasion. She wanted to look extra good that night for Christopher. Of course, she also wanted to look good in case they ran into Kendra. Otherwise she might report back to Christopher's whole family that he was engaged to some total slob. Of course, Aisha realized, she had no idea of who exactly it was who constituted Christopher's family. There was so much she didn't know, and he was so secretive about his past.

41

As she ducked out the door of the bathroom Aisha ran smack into Zoey and Lucas, who were walking arm in arm, licking each other's snow cones.

"You guys!" teased Aisha. "How corny can you get?"

"You don't want to know. Where's Christopher?" Zoey asked.

Aisha looked around. "He was supposed to be waiting for me here, actually. You haven't seen him?"

They both shook their heads.

"We'll wait with you. He probably ran to the bathroom himself. Eesh—Lucas thinks he's being followed by a fortune-teller."

"Excuse me, Zoey, but I *know* I'm being followed." Lucas proceeded to tell Aisha a long, convoluted story of how a strange fortune-teller with a black veil cornered him near the entrance and demanded he get a fortune, but Aisha was having trouble listening. Where could be taking Christopher so long?

Zoey tried unsuccessfully to finish the two snow cones before they melted into her hand. She ran to dump them in the trash, signaling to Lucas to stop the story until she returned. Aisha, meanwhile, shifted uncomfortably and glanced at her watch.

"Hey, Eesh!" Zoey called. "Christopher's right there! Look, he's just getting on the roller coaster now—with—with . . ."

Aisha looked. "Kendra?" Her heart sank. Why was he being so sneaky?

Six

"Lucas, c'mon! What are you doing?" Zoey had Lucas's hand in hers and was dragging him down the aisle to the cotton candy vendor. Her face was bright red from screaming on the Tilt-A-Whirl.

Lucas stared behind him into the night. He looked past the drunk, laughing couples and shrieking kids.

"Lucas?" Zoey stopped pulling and came closer. "Did you see a ghost or something?"

"It's so weird. I keep seeing that fortune-teller chick. I swear to God she's following me. She was just right there." He pointed to a spot a few yards behind them, now occupied by a cackling clown painting faces.

"She probably thinks you're so cute, you need your fortune read," Zoey teased. "Don't worry, I'll protect you from the big, bad fortune-teller. But first . . . I'm going to attack some cotton candy!" Zoey ran for the cart, leaving Lucas standing there, perplexed. He felt sure it was the same fortune-teller. Why was she following him? It didn't make sense that she was trying to drum up business. It was hardly good business smarts to follow one potential customer around all night. No, he was certain that she'd picked him, of all people. For what? Could it be that she was a real

43

fortune-teller, not just out to make a buck, and that she knew something about him? A belief in superstition had been bred in Lucas as strongly as a belief in hard work. It was part of the Cabral tradition, part of the fishing mens' tradition, part of the Portuguese tradition. . . .

Lucas shrugged and turned toward where Zoey stood paying for her cotton candy. Reaching her arms up to the cashier, Zoey inadvertently pulled her thin miniskirt tighter around her hips so that Lucas could see the outline of her underwear. He grinned. With a girlfriend as sexy as Zoey, a guy had to think he was blessed with some kind of good fortune. Maybe all that Cabral superstition had paid off. He sneaked up behind her and cleared his throat, lowering his voice an octave. "Pssst . . . hey, little lady, how'd ya like to ride the Tunnel of Love?"

Zoey whirled around, swatting Lucas with a headful of silky blond hair. "Lucas, you better watch it. Next time you'll get more in your face than my hair! I think you've managed to freak me out talking about your weird fortune-teller."

Lucas smiled. He felt so much better here with Zoey than he had all week, slaving on the fishing boat, then coming home to his father's muttered oaths and complaints. Lucas scooped Zoey into his arms and twirled her around. He gracefully maneuvered her kicking feet around a gang of kids waiting in line for the cotton candy and finally let her down slowly into his arms. "Zoey, I'm so lucky to have a girlfriend like you. Even if you are deserting me for California."

"Lucas, I appreciate your sudden burst of romance, and I'm choosing to ignore the California bit—but I will inform you that you put me down right on a gob of gum, and now it's all over my high-tops." Zoey

44

made a face and tried to balance holding one foot in her hand to inspect the damage. Lucas steadied her. He couldn't help thinking it was fated for him to ruin her high-tops since he'd just been lusting after the way she looked in them. Lucas loved Zoey's casual sexiness. Unlike Claire, who would overdo a sexy skirt by wearing heels, Zoey had the exquisite sense to wear funky sneakers with a teeny mini, and this was one of the reasons Lucas found her so irresistible. He kissed her.

"Zo—you look so sexy in your high-tops, I'm probably getting punished by the gods for ogling you."

"Oh, you've been thinking about that fortune-teller too much," Zoey snapped. "Stay here while I run to the bathroom and wash the gum slime off my shoe."

Lucas watched Zoey make her way through the crowd toward the bathrooms. Though she was a total romantic, Lucas knew Zoey had no patience for New Age superstition and religious philosophies. She was too much of an optimist to believe in divine punishment and fate. But he, on the other hand, was not only susceptible to beliefs like these, he was attracted to them.

"Lucas . . ."

The voice confused him. It wasn't Aisha's voice, or Claire's, or Nina's. . . . He looked around. Kate? Could it be Kate? No, she couldn't have such a low, strangely lilting tone. Where was it coming from? On either side of him were families, herding their youngsters into a manageable clump lest they scamper off and get lost. In front of him was the midway aisle, but he recognized none of the people streaming by. Behind him was a closed and shuttered vendor's wagon. He paused. Unless . . .

"Lucas, I know your story. Don't you want me to tell it?"

That was it. *The voice was coming from inside the closed wagon!*

Lucas spun around. It was the fortune-teller. It had to be. He dodged over to the back of the wagon, looking for an entrance. The door was locked. Lucas jostled the handle and pulled at the door, but it wouldn't give. "Why are you following me? How do you know my name?" he cried anxiously, kicking at the door.

"Here, look up."

Above the door and to the left was a sliding window, and Lucas watched incredulously as it slid partially open. A dim green light spilled on to his face. He blinked.

A veiled figure appeared at the window, illuminated by the strange green glow. Lucas was staring at the obscured face of the fortune-teller. A shudder ran through him. What could she want with him? He threw back his shoulders and drew himself up tall.

"How do you know my name?" Lucas demanded. In the background the cacophony of noises of the carnival—tinkling music, squealing children—seemed to drop to a tiny murmur.

"I know everything about you. Come to me and I'll tell you. I know your destiny." She bowed her head and started to slide the window shut.

"Wait!" Lucas cried. "Where are you going? What if I *do* want to have my fortune read?"

But the window was shut, and she didn't speak. Lucas wiped his sweaty palms on his pants. What had she said? Something about his destiny? He stared at the wagon, as if looking hard enough at it might summon the mysterious fortune-teller. He knew deep down in his heart that now he *had* to get his fortune

46

read. It was only a matter of letting her find him again. *And that shouldn't take too long,* he thought as he walked back around to the front of the wagon, his stomach knotted with excitement.

Zoey was standing at the spot where she'd left him, looking concerned. Her face brightened when she saw him. "Lucas! I lost you—what happened?"

Lucas hesitated. Would Zoey believe him? Would she be frightened? He swallowed.

"Zo—she knows my name." Lucas's face was pale.

"I can't believe it. Lucas . . . did you go see that fortune-teller again? What *is* going on? What do you mean, she *knows* your name?" Zoey took Lucas's hands in hers and stared at him as though he were crazy. "Lucas, is this some kind of joke?"

He shook his head.

"I can tell it's not, from your face." Her voice softened, but she continued to look at him searchingly. Lucas told her what happened, purposefully leading her away from the wagon as he spoke. Zoey listened and then pondered for a few moments. Lucas watched her brow furrow in concentration.

"Lucas," Zoey began, still nibbling at the remains of her cotton candy absently, "you say she's been following us all night. Why couldn't she have overheard me call your name? I mean, I know you think—want—her to be a real psychic, but I think the whole thing is probably an elaborate spoof to get a few fortunes read. Who knows, the carnival managers might pay her to follow people around for added thrills. I mean, it does give me the creeps. It really does—" She shivered and glanced back at the wagon. "I just think the whole thing is a stupid gimmick to get business."

Lucas nodded. Maybe Zoey was right. A part of

him felt disappointed, but he was forced to admit that Zoey's reasoning made sense. Anyone could overhear his name being called, that was for sure. And if it was something more than an aggressive sales pitch, he'd soon know it. In the meantime, here he was with Zoey on a rare night out and he ought to make the best of it.

"Let's go through the haunted house and forget about it. If she shows up again—weeelll—she shows up. This time you better not be in the bathroom." He elbowed Zoey gently in the side. She giggled, and they strode down the midway hand in hand. Lucas asked a ticket seller where they could find the haunted house.

"Haunted house?" The old man scratched his head quizzically. "Oh, you mean the Transylvanian Terror Train. It's right past the Zipper next to the Monkey Barrel." He pointed to a lane skirting off to the left.

"Lucas?" Zoey asked as they headed off. "Why do I get the feeling that Transylvanian Terror Train means Gropeage in the Dark in Lucas language?"

Lucas brushed his hair out of his eyes and made an ironic face. "Zoey, I hate to disappoint you, but the Lucas I know will be too terrified to make any passes. But as I mentioned before, we could always go on the Tunnel of Love—I'm sure that's where we'd find Nina and Benjamin."

"Oh, I don't know about that," Zoey said flatly. "Benjamin's not likely to want to spend any more time in the dark. Oh, Lucas, look, there it is!"

She pointed to a huge gray sign spelling out Transylvanian Terror Train in black gothic lettering. Neon drops of blood dripped off the bottom of each letter. A long line of people led up to the entrance of the ride, which was a gaping vampire mouth with fangs that opened and closed to let the train enter.

Lucas hooted and bit Zoey on the neck. "Kiss of death. Did I ever tell you that I'm actually a vampire? I've been living off your blood for months now."

"You wish," retorted Zoey, guiding Lucas firmly to the back of the line. "Look at the people getting off the ride. Their faces look kinda drained of blood. I don't know, Lucas. . . ." She pretended to shiver. "Should we dare ride the Terror Train?"

When the ticket taker opened the door to their compartment, Lucas looked around a last time for the fortune-teller. She didn't appear to be in the vicinity. He wondered briefly if he was so tired from working on the boat that he'd hallucinated the whole thing. He scowled at the thought of working on the boat. *I'd rather take tickets for carnival rides than end up an overworked, exhausted fisherman.*

Zoey poked Lucas in the side, and their train lurched to a start. "Hey, isn't that your fortune lady over there talking to the train guy? Wasn't she wearing a black veil?"

Lucas craned his neck, but their train pulled into the vampire mouth and was swallowed up by darkness before he could see anything. For a moment they heard the sound of heavy, raspy breathing.

"That's supposed to be the vampire . . . ," Zoey whispered.

"Duhhhh . . ." Lucas giggled. "This is gonna be cool." The train slowed to a crawl.

"Uh-oh!" someone screamed behind them. The train dropped abruptly, and a bright white light flashed, illuminating a vampire in a glass case. A young girl squealed in fright. Zoey gasped as the cavern went black and a whoosh of cold air blasted them.

"What is this, a car wash or a haunted house?" Lucas muttered. Beneath them the train lurched sickeningly around a curve and then slowed as they approached a glowing red door. From behind the door came hysterical screams and thumping noises. As the train neared the door it flew open to reveal a woman clutching her neck while a gigantic vampire tore her throat into strips with his claws.

"Gross . . . that looks real." Zoey groaned. Lucas put his arm around her protectively.

The train made several sharp turns and they dodged a bunch of fake bats that flew at them until it slowed again before a waterfall. A low, accented voice over the loudspeaker announced the "Vampire's Bloodbath."

"Prepare to ride beneath a waterfall of blood of the vampire's victims. . . . Do not, I repeat, do not touch the blood, or you will ride the Transylvanian Terror Train for life, condemned to become the vampire's next victim."

"Aw, it's raspberry Kool-Aid," Lucas whispered in Zoey's ear. "Maybe we should hop the car when we're underneath the waterfall and have a romantic moment together."

"Lucas!" Zoey yelped. For a second Lucas thought she was reacting to his crazy suggestion. But then he heard the other passengers gasp and shout. Zoey was motioning at a figure that had emerged from outside the waterfall. Now it was stepping through the water toward the train, which had slowed to give passengers the full claustrophobic effect of being trapped behind sheets of red water.

"Lucas, it's her, I swear it's her!"

Lucas stared in shock as the person moved closer to their car. The black veil was now drenched, as was the gypsy robe, but there was no denying that it was the fortune-teller. She stopped and raised her arms dramatically, letting the water spill over her body. As their car passed she looked at Lucas and spoke.

"Meet me in ten minutes at Malvolia's House of Secrets . . . Lucas."

Behind them a girl's voice piped up. "Is she real? Is that part of the show, Daddy?"

Zoey clenched Lucas's forearm. Before either of them had a chance to react, the train snaked away through more twists and turns. When they emerged into daylight, Lucas leaped out, pulling a startled Zoey with him. Lucas was conscious of other passengers staring at him as they hurried off, but he didn't have time to care. What he needed was to find Malvolia's House of Secrets. Now.

"Lucas, what's going on? What are you doing?" Zoey cried.

"Look, Zo—I've got to find out what this is all about. I'm going to get my fortune read. I want you to round up everyone else and meet me there, at Malvolia's House of Secrets. Please?" He pushed the hair out of her eyes and kissed her forehead. "Please, Zoey? I've got to do this."

She sighed heavily. "Lucas, I'm worried. This whole thing has gone too far. I do think it's wise to round up our friends, but can't you wait until then?"

Lucas looked into her eyes. Something told him he wanted to be alone. "Zo, just meet me there," he murmured, and then he was off, running to the booth where he'd first seen the fortune-teller.

As he expected, she was waiting for him. Although her hair was dripping wet, she had changed into a new robe and veil. She stood against the back wall of the booth—legs crossed, chin lowered, eyes mysteriously shadowed. When she saw him, she nodded slowly and beckoned for him to enter the little booth. Lucas felt the hair on the back of his neck rise. He sat down on a couch facing a table with a crystal ball and a deck of tarot cards. She didn't move but stood watching him, a small smile playing on her lips.

"Hello, Lucas."

"Hello, Malvolia. Is that what I should call you?" Lucas strained to keep his voice sounding natural and confident.

"That's fine. You knew you had to come, didn't you? And where's your little girlfriend; she's coming, isn't she?"

Lucas wondered why the fortune-teller cared where Zoey was. For an instant he was almost annoyed.

"Oh, yeah, she's coming, with the rest of our friends—"

"The rest of your friends?" Her voice was sharp.

"Oh, is that okay? I mean, we can go ahead and do my fortune now. . . ." Lucas felt nervous. She was acting a little weird.

"Of course, of course . . ." The fortune-teller smiled and crossed the room to sit down on the chair across from him. "And it's perfect that your girlfriend's bringing friends. They shall all have their fortunes read. Really, it's wonderful; I was just a little surprised. . . ."

There was a pause. Lucas stared awkwardly at the Indian bangles she wore around her wrist. Looking into her veiled eyes made him uncomfortable.

"Lucas, shall we begin?" Her voice had become soft and husky, nearly a whisper. "As you know, I've been following you all night. From the moment I saw you, I was struck by your energy. I knew everything

52

about you. You have very strong energy for a fortune-teller. What that means is that you have a *very* strong destiny." She paused and fingered a carved wooden lighter on the table. "Do you mind if I smoke?"

Lucas shook his head. He felt slightly dizzy.

"Lucas, I see an island." She exhaled smoke slowly from her cigarette. "An island. Small. Maybe nearby this place." She held up her hand and slowly gestured in a huge circle. The bangles fell abruptly down to the bottom of her wrist, tinkling loudly. Lucas flinched. If the fortune-teller noticed, she didn't show it. Instead she looked past him and blew three perfect smoke rings that floated over his shoulder and disintegrated.

"An island. A man is there. Older. Traditional. Your father?" She glanced at him, her eyebrows raised.

"Yes, my father," Lucas croaked.

"Your future is this man's future. You will never leave this island. You are destined to the island. Do you understand me?"

Lucas gasped. Had he expected this? He felt as if he had been hit by a rock. Deep down in his heart he realized suddenly that he'd known all along what the fortune-teller would say and why. His worst nightmare had come true.

Seven

"So you say he's gone nutso over a fortune-teller?" Christopher Shupe strode purposefully down the midway, piecing together the confused story that a breathless Zoey had hysterically relayed. Christopher's crisis reflexes were sharp, and so it had fallen to him to gather up the gang and lead them to Malvolia's House of Secrets.

"Zoey, are you saying that this fortune-teller was following Lucas *into* the haunted house?" Aisha asked.

"Yo, Aish, cool all the questions," Christopher interjected. "Zoey's obviously freaked out. Nina—" He held out a warning finger to Nina, who looked as though she were about to burst apart with suggestions. "So lemme sum it up, Zo," he continued. "You tell me if I've got it right—Lucas got obsessed with a weird fortune-teller who followed him around all evening calling him by name. We are now on our way to her booth to meet him, extract him from a boiling cauldron of witches' blood—if necessary—and get our fortunes read on the way out? Cool! That's what I call a bargain." He winked at Jake and Benjamin, who were stifling giggles.

"Jerk." Aisha pouted. "You're making fun of

Zoey." She put a protective arm around her friend, who was urging them all to go faster.

"Maybe Lucas has been kidnapped by a Satan worshiper!" Nina piped up, exchanging knowing looks with Benjamin.

"Oh, watch out for the power of suggestion," retorted Christopher. "All right, guys, here we are. Let's go in cool."

Malvolia's House of Secrets was a small pink shack painted with stars and moons. A tinted green window revealed Lucas sitting on a couch, cradling his head in his arms.

"Lucas?" Zoey called. She rushed inside. Christopher followed closely behind.

"Lucas, are you okay? What happened?" Zoey knelt beside him and lifted his head. Lucas shook, as if he'd been suddenly disturbed from somewhere deep inside himself. He gave them a tight smile.

"Oh, hey, you guys. Glad to see you made it. May I introduce Malvolia?"

They all turned as a robed and bejeweled woman emerged from behind a scarlet curtain.

"Well," she said. She gave them a theatrical smile from behind her lacy veil. "Well, well, well. What wonderful friends you have, Lucas. So supportive." She pronounced her *s*'s exaggeratedly, almost hissing. "We're a little cramped here, as you can tell. Why don't you all go outside and come in one at a time for your fortunes?"

Lucas stood up quickly. "Great idea. C'mon, guys." He began to herd them outside. But Christopher stayed put, watching Malvolia closely.

"I think I'll stay here, if that's okay. . . ." He sat down on the couch. He wondered what exactly had gone on between Lucas and Malvolia. Lucas seemed to be terribly moved but trying hard not to show it. He was acting like Malvolia's agent or something—as if he wanted to prove to them he wasn't afraid of her. Out of the corner of his eye Christopher glanced at Malvolia. She had moved back to let everyone out and was standing at the entrance, watching them confer excitedly with Lucas, who kept shaking his head. Christopher noticed she was staring at Kate in particular. *Weird,* he thought. He waved at Aisha, who was looking at him with concern.

"That boy . . . yes, you—" Malvolia pointed at Jake. "You'll go first."

"Me? Me?" Jake's mouth fell open. Kate, standing next to him, smiled. She pushed him toward the door. "Go on, Jake. Fortunes are fun. You'll get a good one, honey."

"Now!" Malvolia said harshly, and whirled around. Christopher saw her face grow sour. He decided she was definitely not someone he liked.

Jake chuckled as he came inside. "I can't believe he's got us all doing this. Crazy Lucas. Mind if I sit next to you, Christopher—or should I refer to you as my bodyguard?"

Malvolia leaned forward and clasped Jake's hands in hers. "Jake."

He grinned expectantly. "Did I tell you my name? Oh, I'm sorry, I'm not supposed to ask questions like that, right?"

Malvolia didn't answer but bowed her head over Jake's hand, moving her lips silently. Suddenly she reacted as if she'd been struck.

"Jake, you are haunted." She spoke fervently. "You are haunted by someone . . . someone . . . who is dead. Someone once very close to you. You will always be haunted by the dead."

56

Christopher was at first too stunned to come to Jake's aid, but he couldn't have done much comforting, anyway. The second her words sank in, Jake leaped from his chair and ran outside. Christopher was left alone with a trembling Malvolia who muttered incoherent phrases over the crystal ball. How could Malvolia know about Wade, Jake's older brother who had died in a drunk-driving accident? Was it possible that she'd seen newspaper clippings, recognized Jake McRoyan from his football publicity? *Not likely,* Christopher thought. Only one other possibility existed, and he of all people, businessman that he was—would be unlikely to believe it. Was Malvolia a real psychic?

Zoey stepped into the booth, her face agitated. "Lu-ucas s-s-said I should come in. . . ." She faltered. "Is that okay?" She looked to Malvolia for agreement.

"Please. Sit down. How pretty you are, and how nice. Everyone likes you, don't they?" It was a strange question, but Christopher had to admit it was a damn good guess. Zoey laughed nervously in response.

"Let's see now." Malvolia stared into her crystal ball and looked up at Zoey, then down again. She frowned.

She sighed deeply. "Your fortune, I'm sorry to say, is not a good one. You have a love now?"

Zoey nodded in assent.

"This love will not be true to you."

"What do you mean?" Zoey cried out, aghast. Malvolia shrugged. She forced a pitying smile. "That's all, honey. I'm sorry. Please get the next person."

Christopher blinked. Lucas not be true to Zoey?

Now it was getting a little crazy. He was almost angry. Why were all the fortunes so terrible? His stomach turned over. What would Malvolia say to Aisha? And would she know *his* own secret? He'd just about decided not to have his fortune read and was getting up to leave when Aisha walked into the shack.

She glanced at Christopher, her forehead lined with worry, as she sat down on the little couch. "Jake and Zoey are totally freaked out," she told Christopher. "Kate's trying to talk to Jake, and Zoey and Lucas are all silent and weird. Nina and Benjamin think the whole thing is stupid, and they won't do it. But Christopher—" Her voice dropped to a whisper. "I had to come in after hearing what she said to Jake. She's the real thing, Christopher!" Christopher managed a feeble smile.

Malvolia smiled at Aisha. "You live in a big house, and many strangers pass through this house, no?"

Aisha nodded, wide-eyed. She nudged Christopher in the side. "You have a younger . . . brother? Yes? All right. In the crystal ball I see . . . I see your love. . . ." Christopher tensed. "But this love belongs to someone else. Someone from his life a long time ago. You are a thief, Aisha. You must go to your love's past to discover his secret. You have stolen—"

Christopher found that he had risen to his feet. His fists were clenched. "A thief? Who are you to call my girlfriend a thief!" He could no longer contain his fury. What was this crazy psychic trying to do, ruin his relationship?

"C'mon, Aisha," he shouted, grabbing her and glaring at Malvolia. "Get the hell away from us!"

Jake and Lucas ran inside the booth. "Christopher, man, cool down." Lucas took him by the arm.

Malvolia glowered at them. "Give me my money!" she spat. "Or I'm calling the security guard on him!" She jabbed a finger at Christopher. "It's not my fault if you're all doomed!"

"Doomed?" Christopher bellowed. "You crazy lady, you . . . you . . ." He shook his fist. Jake and Lucas pushed him out the door, leaving a wad of bills on the table for Malvolia. "Easy there, Christopher, easy . . ." Jake patted him on the back. "She's crazy, don't worry about it, c'mon."

Everyone had rushed to the door after Jake and Lucas, and now they moved back to let Aisha, Christopher, Jake, and Lucas through. Malvolia disappeared behind the scarlet curtain.

Aisha was crying, and Zoey tried to comfort her while Lucas talked to Christopher.

"Look, let's just laugh this whole thing off, okay?" It was Jake, trying to be the voice of reason. "It's no big deal. So we got a little spooked. Some crazy lady went psycho on us. There's no way some chick in a pink booth could know our futures. She probably just has some standard lines she uses to get a rise out of people. Let's just move on and go to another ride, huh? We're at the carnival—it's Friday night—let's enjoy it!"

"I second the motion!" Nina exclaimed. "You guys are letting a weird old lady with menopause get to you. So she knew about Wade, about the island, about the Grays' B&B—so she's been to Chatham Island, read some newspapers, so what?"

Christopher wanted to believe Nina, but his heart was still pounding from fright. Maybe it was impossible to really shed your past; maybe that was what was freaking him out so much. *Going on the roller coaster again will cool me down,* he thought. He turned to Aisha and gave her a hug. "Oh, baby, that lady was talking such crap. You are the true owner of my heart."

"Excuse me, folks." It was a security guard. He was staring hard at Christopher, though he addressed the entire group. Malvolia stood next to him, smiling triumphantly. "But I'm afraid I'm going to have to ask you all to leave the carnival premises."

Eight

Claire's heart beat faster as she and Steven approached her front door. She knew Aaron would be watching for her return, waiting for the moment when he could eavesdrop on her doorstep drop-off. She wanted to put on a good show. It was tricky—Aaron mustn't think she guessed he was there; her actions had to seem natural.

The moment had arrived. Claire turned to face Steven. "It was *so* nice meeting you." She projected her voice, hoping it would carry through the front door. She smiled sweetly at Steven. He was staring at her, taking in the white silk tank top outlining her breasts, the shiny black hair tumbling over her shoulders, the tight black jeans. Claire guessed he was thinking it was the last evening he'd ever spend with such a beautiful girl. And despite the several instances in which she'd bruised his ego, she thought she'd done a remarkably good job of remaining civil.

"Claire—the pleasure was all mine. *Really.* I mean, what a sharpshooter you are. And beautiful, I mean, you're just, well," his voice cracked, "so beautiful."

"Uh-huh." Claire waited. She opened the front door a crack and left her hand on the knob. *He won't leave without making some kind of bad pass.*

"Do you, uh, think we could, um, I don't know how to say this. . . ." He laughed nervously.

Claire could practically hear Aaron's breathing. Her heart was in her throat. She moistened her lips and looked up at Steven.

"Oh, Claire . . ." Steven dove down onto her, practically crushing her against his chest. His hands fumbled with the back of her head, trying to maneuver her face into his.

Claire pushed him back roughly. "What," she spat, "are you doing?" Her eyes flashing with scorn, she wiped the saliva from her mouth and made a face. "You have a lot of nerve, Steven. Good night." Throwing a poisonous backward glance, she slammed the door behind her.

Once inside the foyer, Claire breathed deeply and stood still, her eyes closed. She waited for Aaron's witty rejoinder.

Nothing. She heard the faint tinkle of voices and laughter, but otherwise there was only silence. No arms slipped around her waist, no hot breath on her neck. Just the sound of Steven's shoes scraping the gravel and then his car engine starting up and accelerating.

Claire opened her eyes. She turned once around, surveying the foyer and entrance hallway. Aaron wasn't there. Her heart sank. What could it mean? How could he not . . . want . . . to know? She bit her lip. Perhaps he was hiding, waiting to see if she showed signs of disappointment. *Clever bastard,* she thought, chiding herself for thinking she could outwit him. Stalling for time, she crossed to the hall mirror and powdered her face. Where were those voices coming from? She could discern Sarah's high, piercing laugh. She pretended to look at herself, all the while watching the room in the mirror for any signs of activity.

Nothing. Claire frowned and then called out, "Daddy? Sarah? I'm home. . . ."

She followed the voices down the hallway. *Maybe something came up with his band,* she decided. *He's probably not home. And Sarah and Daddy are having friends over for cocktails.*

"Yes! It's a horse, horse . . . no . . ." It was her father's voice. Were they playing some kind of game?

"Try again, try again . . ." A strange female voice.

"Pig, no, horse, antelope? Gazelle? Oh! Oh!" Sarah's voice, brimming over with excitement.

"C'mon, Mom." Now Claire could hear Aaron's voice ringing clearly over the other voices. She winced.

"Aaron?" Claire opened the door to the living room.

"Claire?" Aaron looked up, dazed. "Back so early?"

"Claire, darling, you're just in time!" Burke gave her a huge smile. "We're playing a fierce game of Pictionary, aren't we, Aaron?"

Aaron laughed, gulping down the rest of a beer. Claire stepped carefully over the threshold. *Since when does he hang out at home, drinking beer with the folks?* she wondered.

"Claire! Hi, sweetie. Did you have a nice time on your date? Come here, I'd like you to meet Lindsay Gordon. She's a friend of Aaron's from school. Lindsay, this is my stepdaughter, Claire."

"What?" Claire stared at Sarah, then at her father, then Aaron. They were all seated cozily around a small table on two sofas. Next to her father a girl rose and smiled at Claire. She offered her hand. "I'm

sorry. A friend from where, did you say, Sarah?"
Claire automatically shook the girl's hand, still staring at Sarah and Aaron. The blood drained from her
face.

"Aaron goes to school with Lindsay," Sarah purred
smoothly.

"Mom ran into her at the grocery store in Weymouth," Aaron mumbled.

"And invited me for a lovely dinner," Lindsay finished with a graceful flourish.

"You're playing, um, Pictionary?" Claire was still
trying to understand what had happened. Other than
her night ending even more miserably than it had
begun.

They all laughed sheepishly. "Lindsay's an artist,
so of course she and your father are winning." Sarah
tittered.

My God, you're merciless, thought Claire. It was
unbelievable. Not only did this girl come to *her* house
for dinner, she took Claire's place on the couch next
to her own father!

"You've got a great family, Claire," Lindsay
offered. Claire threw her the iciest smile she could
muster.

"Oh, yes, as you can see, they're a dream." She
glared at her father and Sarah, ignoring Aaron altogether. She felt as though her heart were breaking.
Was he complicitous with Sarah and Burke? What
was his problem? If only he had the balls to stand up
and kiss her, throw his arms around her, tell her he
loved her in front of their parents and this butt-kiss-
ing girl. Claire wondered if Lindsay had a huge
crush on Aaron.

"Claire, uh, why don't you sit down?" Burke
sounded wary.

"How was the carnival? Why don't you tell us about it?" Sarah swished the ice in her drink and inspected her fingernail polish.

"Yeah, Claire. Give us the dirt." Aaron leaned back and put his hands behind his head. He took another swig of beer.

"Oh, gee, I don't know. It sounds as if a mere roller-coaster ride couldn't beat the Pictionary game you guys have going on here. I did some good rifle shooting, though. Actually I won such a big stuffed animal, I couldn't carry it home. Pity, I'm sure it would look great sitting on the couch right there next to Dad." She paused to let that one hit home. Then she turned to face Lindsay.

"So how do you like boarding school?" The question came out sounding as though she'd asked Lindsay about the army. Lindsay, however, didn't flinch and looked Claire in the eye. Claire summed her up in one casual glance. She was definitely pretty, but in a bland sort of way. She had blue eyes and a chin-length blond bob. *One of those girls who looks like she goes to prep school,* Claire noted. She wore an elegant, tailored light blue skirt and matching jacket with pearls. Claire could tell from her demeanor that she was accustomed to socializing in sophisticated circles and getting what she wanted out of these same circles. What Claire couldn't tell, however, was how Lindsay felt about Aaron. It made her uneasy. Would Aaron fall for a girl like this? Claire knew *Sarah* already had.

"Boarding school is a delight. Really. It gets such a bad rap, but it's actually a lot of fun. But I'm sure you've heard all about our crazy school from Aaron." She gave Aaron a pointed smile.

"It must be hard, though." Claire's eyes glittered.

"Your social life is so limited. I guess you have to resort to being palmed off on guys by their own mothers. Must make things rough." She, too, turned to Aaron and smiled sweetly.

"Well." Lindsay faltered. Claire had won. The room was suddenly thick with tension. "I don't have that problem. I meet people lots of ways. In fact," she looked at her watch, "I'm supposed to meet some friends in Weymouth in half an hour. I've got to get going. But it's been a lovely evening." She stood up.

Burke and Sarah were slow to respond. But Aaron, sneering at Claire, leaped up and offered to escort Lindsay out. Sarah and Burke followed them, Sarah trying to cover the tension by making overly animated small talk. Claire stayed seated, seething with fury at her "family."

"Jealous much?" Aaron returned to the living room alone. He shook his head at her in disgust.

Claire didn't say anything.

"You might have been a bit more graceful. I did my best to handle the situation gracefully."

"You sure did!" Claire hissed.

The two were glaring at each other in silence when Burke stormed into the room, followed by a frazzled Sarah.

"Claire, this is just too much!"

"What is? I am forced out on a date with a total drip who practically paws me on my front door, and then I find Sarah has conspired to bring some girl home without my knowing it and I find her here, throwing herself at Aaron, *in my own home.* You're right, Dad, this has gone too far." She slammed her fist down on the table and then strode out of the room.

Fifteen minutes later Claire heard a knock on her door. She was crying into the pillow, reliving the

66

night in her head. She roused herself and went to the door. It was Aaron.

"You? I thought they wouldn't let you up here. And you always follow the rules and regulations."

"Claire, look. I'm sorry for being a jerk, but you've also got to stop acting like a jealous brat. This whole situation is ridiculous and crazy, and we just have to grit our teeth and get through it as calmly as we can." He smiled and took her in his arms. "Poor baby. How could you get all riled up about Lindsay Gordon? You took her out pretty bad. She'll never let me forget it." He snickered.

"It was in my own home. . . ." She moaned. "My own home."

Aaron gently kissed her on the mouth. He led her over to her bed. "You put on your sexiest nightgown while I tell you my idea. I won't watch you undress, of course."

Claire's shoulders relaxed. The whole night had exhausted her. All she wanted to do was go to bed. "Forget the sexy nightgown," she pouted. I'm wearing my red flannel." She rifled through her drawers and produced a tattered but comfortable nightie. She put it on over her shirt and then took her clothing off underneath.

Aaron watched, fascinated. "How do girls do that?" he asked.

"Easy," Claire answered. "Coed summer camp."

Aaron put an arm around her. "I wish I could be your bunkmate," he whispered.

"Shhh. None of that. I'm still mad at you." But she could already feel herself melting. "Tell me your idea."

"Look, I know how to placate my mom. All I need to do is go on a date with someone once, come home, and tell her I'm madly in love with you and nothing and no one can change my mind."

That's what I wanted to hear. Claire got under the covers and put her head on Aaron's lap.

"Promise?"

"Promise."

Lara threw down her veil and tore off her robe. She unclipped the black wig and ran a finger through her short blond hair. She hurriedly scrubbed off the white pancake makeup that had disguised her facial features. In ten minutes she completed the transformation from Malvolia, the gypsy fortune-teller, back into Lara, girl in blue jeans and Motorhead T-shirt.

She knew she had been a smashing success.

It was a breeze.

Nobody can call me a bad actress. She felt like a Jodie Foster or a Jennifer Jason Leigh. She felt like she should get an Oscar for Best Actress and Best Revenge. Sweet revenge. Fun revenge. Flawless revenge.

But now it was time to hurry and get her grades, so to speak. It was time to follow the Brat Pack home. It was time to eavesdrop on their debriefing session. She wanted to savor every tiny, miserable reaction. She would see the full effects of her fine performance on her unwitting audience.

Lara closed down her precious booth and left the carnival by the back gate.

"Nina, are you really going to tell me that Malvolio, or whatever her name is, just happened to have her Filofax chockful of information about the occupants of Chatham Island?" Aisha demanded. They were all loitering in the parking lot outside the carnival. Jake sat next to Kate on the hood of his car, facing Aisha and Christopher, who leaned up against Christopher's junker. Nina, Benjamin, and Zoey sat cross-legged on the pavement between the two cars. Lucas was a few paces off, staring moodily at the flickering lights of the carnival. Nina puffed on an unlit cigarette, pausing occasionally to blow fake smoke in Benjamin's face.

None of them saw Lara creep up and crouch down behind the tire of the car next to Jake's. She could see everyone but Lucas. Her eyes darted from face to face and then rested on Aisha.

"I mean, I can see how she might have known about the B&B or Kalif. But Kendra? How could anyone know about Kendra?"

Christopher started violently. "Aisha? Just what are you trying to say? That lady made no reference to Kendra. She threw the oldest trick in the book at you—telling you I belonged to someone else—and you obviously bought it hook, line, and sinker!"

"She said to go to your past!" Aisha burst out. Her voice was as miserable as it was defiant. "How could it be mere coincidence? Your sister shows up, and you don't even introduce me until I practically force you to. Then you're all secretive and sneaky, and you won't even let me have two words with her. I mean, what am I supposed to think?" Tears of frustration ran down her face.

From her hiding place Lara smiled. *I knocked Aisha right out.*

"Guys, guys. C'mon," Benjamin pleaded. "Aisha, listen. You've got to admit the only information she really has on you is stuff that's readily available to the public. Don't work yourself up about it. A nasty old lady just had fun at your expense. That's all."

"Christopher, you're shaken up by that lady, too. I know, I could tell from your face the second I sat down next to you on her couch." Aisha sniffled.

"I was shaken up. The whole thing did get to me; you're right. I'm not satisfied by Nina's explanation. But . . ." Christopher let the sentence hang.

"It doesn't make sense. She *picked* us, right? Why would she want to get us?" Jake asked.

"She picked *me*," Lucas broke in gruffly. "She *knew* me. She was the real thing, and you guys don't want to admit it."

Lara's heart beat faster.

"Lucas, please tell me what she told you. Please," Zoey begged.

Lucas was silent.

"Lucas?" Zoey's voice had a plaintive note. "Lucas, if you think she's right, then what do you have to say about *my* fortune?"

Ha. Lara snickered. Score two for Lara. Lucas, busted.

"Oh, Zoey, chill," Nina interjected quickly. "You're letting Lucas freak you out. You think Mr. Lucas My-life-revolves-around-Zoey Cabral could be untrue? That old lady just wishes he would!" Benjamin chuckled at Nina's joke.

"Zoey, I don't know what to say about your fortune. Maybe she meant it this way: *Your* love will not be true. Like, your love for me will not be true. That's kinda how I heard it. You're leaving me for California. Maybe that's what she was talking about."

Lucas walked between a few cars and stood before Zoey, Nina, and Benjamin. Lara ducked underneath the car. She didn't want to take any chances when things were going so well.

"Lucas, how terrible!" Zoey shook her head and

70

reached out a hand to him. "Don't say things like that. Why are you taking all this so personally? Maybe the lady really is crazy. Maybe she's mentally imbalanced, and you happened to be the person she latched on to. That's as likely as any of the other explanations."

"Then how did she know I live on an island? How did she know about my father?" Lucas demanded.

"She's seen you around, she bought fish from your father, she knows who you are—maybe that's why she followed you around in the first place."

"And she contracted food poisoning from your father's fish and went crazy," Nina teased.

"Yeah . . . that makes sense . . . ," Jake said slowly. "If she knows Lucas's family, she's sure to know the rest of us. And Wade, well, his death is no secret."

A silence ensued. In the distance the noises of the carnival mingled with the clanging of boats on the wharf. Lara held her breath. Had it occurred to even one of them that the fortune-teller might be Lara in disguise? If not, was it because they wouldn't think her capable of a such an imaginative and cleverly executed plan or because they themselves weren't clever or imaginative enough to figure it out? She shifted, adjusting her weight. The fact that her name hadn't even been *mentioned* annoyed her.

"Do any of you guys really believe in ESP?" Jake asked finally.

"I do," said Kate softly.

Benjamin grunted in agreement. "But I don't believe old ladies in carnival booths have ESP. That's for sure. Although I will admit this is a striking example of coincidence or con artistry or both."

"What about the rest of you? Zoey? Aisha? Christopher?"

Lara leaned forward. She was dying to hear Zoey's answer.

But it was Christopher who spoke first. "Yesterday I would have said no. Hell, no. Today? I'd have to say—I don't know." He sounded defensive, as if he was embarrassed to admit his newfound ambivalence.

Aisha sighed loudly. "I don't want to answer that question right now. I don't even want to think about that question right now. But I will say this: I'd rather be a thief than find out Christopher's a liar." She glared at him.

Christopher grimaced. Everyone shifted their attention to Zoey.

"Zoey?" Jake raised an eyebrow.

Zoey looked around at all of them helplessly. Her eyes lingered on Lucas, who moved next to Christopher and leaned up against the passenger's seat of the car. He looked gravely back at her.

"I—I—" Zoey stammered. "Hey, why are you all looking at me? You're making me nervous."

Because, Lara thought, *they all rely on you to tell them what's right and wrong. You're the center of their little world, in one way or another. You're Miss Journalist who's always telling everybody what to think.*

But Zoey surprised Lara by not saying anything. Instead she stood up and threw her arms around Lucas. "Lucas, I'm not going to let a fortune-teller scare me away from you."

"Yeeeeaaaaah!" Nina and Benjamin clapped. "Love prevails!"

Lara scowled. Disgusting. She consoled herself with the thought that Zoey's fortune had been the least substantiated. Knowing Jake and Lucas as she did, it was easy to play into their worst fears. Overhearing the snatch of conversation at the Passmores' restaurant had given her the key to Aisha's heart. But Zoey? Well, Lara couldn't be at all sure Lucas would be untrue. She only hoped he would.

Nine

Aisha couldn't sleep. She looked at the clock radio and groaned. Twenty past eight. A Saturday morning from hell. She'd had four, maybe five hours of sleep at the most. Even in the warmth of the June sunshine she was spooked by memories of her nightmares. She rummaged through the drawer of the bedside table for her journal. Writing the dreams down was sometimes the only way to shake them off. She opened the journal to a fresh page and began.

1 In the first dream I'm walking with Christopher through the carnival. He keeps telling me not to turn around. Pleading, beseeching me not to turn around. Is there something behind us, Christopher? I ask. He stares straight ahead and orders me not to look. I finally can't stand it, and when I think he's not pay-

ing attention, I turn around. An old, bent woman in a blood spattered robe trails behind us. When she sees me, she shrieks, "You thief, you thief!" She raises her veil, and I see who it is: Kendra. Christopher disappears, and a crowd gathers around me and Kendra. She grabs me and shouts "thief" over and over.

2. In the next dream I'm happily riding the Ferris wheel with Christopher until it starts going faster and faster, and I ask Christopher what's going on, and he looks down and sees the fortune-teller has taken over the controls. Every time we go around the bottom, she brandishes a knife and tries to slice us. I'm screaming, and the Ferris wheel is going faster and faster until I'm sure it's going to collapse and kill us both.

3 I'm shopping in a store in Weymouth with Loey and Nina. I fall in love with an expensive dress I can't afford. I take it into the dressing room with me and stuff it in my purse. A strange feeling has come over me that I can't resist: I have to steal the dress. I open the door to the dressing room and Kendra's standing there, a disgusted look on her face. "I know you stole the dress," she whispers. "I'm going to tell the saleslady and your friends, and I'm going to warn my brother, Christopher, about you." I start to cry.

Aisha read the dreams over and shook her head. *Boy, did I have a bad night.* Her stomach churned. She looked at the clock again. Christopher would be awake, preparing to leave for his shift at Jimmy's. Suddenly she knew what she had to do.

Jumping out of bed, she quickly pulled on sweats, a T-shirt, and her gym sneakers. She brushed her teeth and splashed cold water on her face. She was hungry, but eating would have to wait.

It was nine o'clock when Aisha walked out of the house, heading for Christopher's apartment.

I've had enough of this, Aisha grumbled to herself. She had to know the truth. How long could Christopher expect her to wait? He'd turned it into an issue of trust, but in the meantime what had happened to respect? It wasn't fair.

Aisha was at the bottom of the stairs of Christopher's building when she heard muffled voices. She froze. Was it Christopher and Kendra? Were they arguing? She placed one sneaker on the wooden stair. It creaked slightly. Grasping the rail to take her weight off her feet, she tiptoed up the stairs. Reaching the top step, she ducked and crawled along the hall until she was beneath Christopher's window. It was open, and the voices she heard were coming from inside.

"Kendra, I'm letting you stay with me. I'm letting you stay here on the island. That's more than I was gonna do. You have to respect my conditions."

"Christopher, she's a nice girl, and for God's sake, you're engaged to her! She'll have to know sometime!"

"Kendra, Aisha *can't* know, ever. Period."

"Aisha can't know what?"

Christopher spun around. Kendra's mouth dropped open.

"Aisha?"

She took a step forward into the apartment, already regretting her outburst. *Damn. If I'd held out for two more minutes, I might have found out what Christopher's hiding from me.* "Christopher, this has gone on long enough. Please tell me what's happening. Is Kendra really your sister?" Aisha demanded.

But Christopher stayed rooted to the spot where he stood. It was Kendra who stepped forward, offering Aisha her hand.

"Aisha, Christopher isn't exactly proud of where he's come from, or of his family, or of me. But I want to be a part of his life now. And I want to get to know you, the woman my brother loves."

Aisha gulped. "Christopher Shupe, for the past two weeks you've been hiding your *sister* from me. Why?"

Christopher hung his head. Kendra giggled. "I'm sorry, Aisha," she said. "It's just that when he gets that hangdog look on his face, I can't help remembering him getting caught throwing spitballs in second grade. He wore that same old expression then."

All three of them burst out laughing. A wave of relief washed over Aisha. "Okay, Kendra, I really do believe you now! Only a bratty little sister tells stories like that." She winked.

"And you!" Aisha pommeled Christopher in the stomach. "So what's your big secret, your—"

"Well . . ." Kendra broke in, glancing nervously at Christopher. He glared at her.

"The big secret's that Kendra's going to be staying here, with me," Christopher said smoothly. "I'm sorry I waited so long to tell you."

"Wait a minute." Aisha sensed something unspoken had passed between the two of them. "That *is* the secret, isn't it? Is something else going on here that I should know about?"

Kendra pursed her lips. "I think I'll take a little walk, all right?" She slipped out the door.

Christopher sat down on the sofa and sighed heavily. Aisha remained standing, her arms crossed.

"Why," she said coldly, "do you insist on keeping everything about your family a secret from me?"

"Aisha, I've told you before: *I put all that behind me*. I don't want to remember my family. I didn't welcome Kendra because I was afraid of the memories and connections she brings with her. Now that you've met her, can't we drop the whole thing? For a while I wasn't sure I would let her stay, so I figured there was no reason for you two to get all buddy-buddy. Now it's decided and she's here to stay, and we'll all be one happy family. Okay?"

Aisha didn't like the sarcastic edge to his voice.

"Are you sure there isn't something else about your past you don't want me to know?"

"Positive," said Christopher firmly. "Positive."

"Uh, Dad?" Jake looked over at his father. It had taken him the entire trip from North Harbor to work up the courage to talk to his dad. Now they were approaching Weymouth High, where Mr. McRoyan was dropping Jake off for his Saturday morning A.A. meeting.

"Yes, Jake? Damn driver!" His father cursed the driver who'd insisted on tailgating for the last mile.

Jake fiddled with the bit of rubber coming loose from the sole of his sneaker. "Dad, do you ever think about ghosts? I mean, do you believe in stuff like that?" he asked. He watched his father carefully out of the corner of his eye.

Mr. McRoyan frowned. "Ghosts? What kind of question is that?" He snorted. "Only the ones that come trick-or-treating on Halloween. Damn it! I speed up, he speeds up. This is ridiculous." He adjusted the rearview mirror.

Jake's throat felt dry. "Dad, I had my fortune read at the carnival last night, and—"

"Fortune read! I'll be darned, you kids into that stuff? I didn't know they still had fortune-tellers at carnivals."

"Of *course,* Dad."

"Did I ever tell you the story about your aunt Helen and how she met Uncle Rick? Aw, wait a minute, here we are. It's a great story; remind me or your mother to tell you. That guy is still following us, amazing! He must be going to your meeting, probably drunk, the fool." Mr. McRoyan's voice harshened. They pulled into the parking lot of Weymouth High, and Mr. McRoyan idled the engine.

"But, uh, Dad? There's something I wanted to tell you."

Mr. McRoyan turned to face Jake. "Son, there's something I want to tell *you.* I know I probably haven't seemed supportive enough of your going to A.A. and all, but I didn't want to get too optimistic too soon. But I think it's time to commend you on what's obviously a commitment to sobriety. I'm proud of you, Jake. You've shown yourself to be strong willed and dedicated. Wade—" His father's voice broke, and he stopped momentarily and looked down. "Wade would be proud, too."

Jake felt a lump in his throat. He opened the car door, avoiding eye contact with his father. He knew if he looked at him, he would start to cry.

I'll talk to him about what happened another time.

"See ya, Dad." Jake hurriedly jumped out of the car.

The meeting had already begun when Jake slipped in. He went immediately to the side table, where someone had brewed up a pot of coffee, and poured himself a cup. The group leader was calling on new people to introduce themselves. Jake wondered if Louise Kronenberger had saved him a seat.

"Yeah, hi. My name's Lara, and I'm an alcoholic."

The plastic foam cup in Jake's hand shook. He set

it down on the table. Lara was here. Jake closed his eyes briefly and lowered his head. It wasn't much of a surprise. In the back of his mind he'd expected to see her one of these mornings. After all, he should be glad for her. But wasn't she supposed to be in rehab somewhere outside of the city? He stirred the sugar in his coffee to stall for time. Facing her wouldn't be easy, not after what she'd done to Kate the night of the prom.

Lara began her introduction. "I just got out of rehab. Well, 'left' would be more like it. I walked away from the place. And I'm coming here because I want to stay sober. But I want to do it on my own, not in someplace where they lock you down at night like you're a criminal. I know we're supposed to talk about serenity today, and I can say I don't know much about that word, not having experienced much of it in my life. But I hope to feel some serenity when I repair the wounds I've made with the people in my life. I've wounded a lot of people."

She looked significantly at Jake, who sat down in the circle. He forced a smile.

"I don't know much about A.A.—like the steps and everything, but I'm sure there are people here who can teach me. For once I'm ready to learn. Thanks." She smiled shyly at the group, then sat down. Jake couldn't help noticing her outfit. It was nothing like her usual Metallica T-shirt and tight black jeans. Today she wore a short peach sundress that showed off her slim legs and bleached blond hair. She looked almost, well, cute. It reminded Jake of something Zoey might wear. Clearly Lara wanted to be a different person. But how he figured in her new identity remained a mystery. He wasn't going to let his guard down anytime soon.

"Lara, we're glad you're here with us. Is there anything else you'd like to share?" the group leader asked.

Lara twiddled with her hair. "Ummm, I don't know. Should I?" She giggled.

"Well, many of us share our current fears and anxieties. We all keep what we call a drunk-a-log. It's kind of a record, a log, of how we resist our substance abuse or how we *don't* resist it enough. You don't have to write anything down. Sharing it here suffices."

Lara nodded. Jake noticed her eyes had glazed over. Was she really paying attention, he wondered, or just pretending?

"Well, I guess I'm worried about replacing my addiction to alcohol with something else. You know, I have a really addictive personality. It's like I'm always going to be addicted to something. So if it's not alcohol, what will it be?" Lara shrugged. "I'm, like, a totally codependent-type person."

Jake coughed to disguise his snicker. Who was Lara kidding? She sounded so smug and insincere, as if she were repeating something she'd read in a magazine article to impress them. But glancing around the circle, he saw everyone nodding empathetically; apparently they *were* taking her seriously. Jake shifted uncomfortably in his chair.

Unable to concentrate, Jake spent the rest of the meeting doodling on a yellow pad and avoiding Lara's inquiring gaze. When it was his turn to share, he passed, explaining that it had been a quiet week. He'd wanted to tell the group about his terrible fortune, but Lara's presence made him self-conscious. But he couldn't avoid her indefinitely. As soon as the meeting broke up, Lara rushed to his side.

"Jake, I know it must be weird to see me here or at all, and I'd appreciate it so much if you would give me a chance to apologize. You're part of the reason I'm here, you know. It was your example. If it hadn't been for you, I wouldn't even know about this meeting."

Jake looked into Lara's eyes. Drunk, she telegraphed her emotions loud and clear. Sober, she was inscrutable. He was momentarily at a loss. How should he relate to this new, sober Lara?

"Lara, I'm sorry, I—I—I don't know how to react. You're so different, and I'm not sure if I should believe you. Are you sorry for running Kate off the road?" Jake crossed his arms and fixed his eyes on her. He searched her face like he searched the football field for a wide receiver.

She looked at her feet. "Oh, Jake. I can't believe the things I did. I can't think of that night without . . ." Her voice trailed off. "Shall we go outside?" When she looked up, Jake saw the tears in her eyes, and he softened. She *was* sorry. Lara McAvoy was sincerely apologizing for pulling one of her trademark stunts. Amazing.

They walked outside together and sat down on a bench. It was a beautiful Saturday morning; the air was crisp and breezy. Jake wondered if Kate was out photographing the old part of Weymouth as she'd mentioned she might be. He hoped so; lately she'd been so moody, she hadn't been leaving the house. As if reading his mind, Lara asked him casually about Kate.

"How are you two doing together? I'm so embarrassed about my jealous fits. God, what was I thinking? You guys are a *great* couple."

Jake couldn't help smiling at the compliment. Lara watched him intently. He felt grateful suddenly that she was there to listen. He hadn't realized how anxious he was.

"Yeah, it's great, we're great. I mean, it's not perfect and all, but you know, I love her. I'm glad we're together."

"You sound as if you're worried about something." Lara flashed a sympathetic smile.

"Yeah, I guess so. Maybe I'm worried about Kate. She's been depressed and moody lately." He laughed nervously. "Uh, is this weird, Lara? Me talking about Kate with you? It's so nice to have someone to talk to."

"Oh, Jake, it's fine, it's no problem. You know I'm your friend. Please." Lara leaned closer to him and crossed her legs demurely.

"Well, I just don't know what to do when she gets all depressed. I don't know if it's my fault or what. And sometimes." He hesitated. "Sometimes she gets kinda needy, too."

"Needy? Hmmm, that's a drag, huh?" Lara nodded, looking into the distance. Jake felt guilty; why was he sitting here talking to Lara about Kate? He decided to change the subject.

"So, Lara, tell me about rehab. What was it like there?"

Lara stiffened at the mention of the word *rehab*. She bristled with indignance. "Jake, you don't know, you just can't imagine what those bastards do to you. They treat you like you're a crazy person or a criminal! You're literally locked up, and they wear the keys, just like a prison guard." She stared up at him, and he was horrified to see tears running down her cheeks.

"Oh, God, Lara, I'm so sorry, that sounds terrible. . . . I, uh . . ." Jake put an arm around her and patted her back awkwardly. Sobbing, she rested her head in his lap.

Jake stared helplessly across the school lawn. A sense of panic overcame him. Why was Lara practically in his lap? Why did he have to be the one to console her when it was the last thing he should be doing? Out of the corner of his eye Jake saw a girl who looked like Kate approach the school. He winced guiltily: It had to be perverse punishment that Kate's double would happen to show up at this very moment. Jake shifted uneasily; the girl did look an awful lot like Kate. In fact, wasn't she swinging a camera case on her arm?

"Jake?"

"Kate?" It was Kate! Jake leaped up from the bench, rudely pushing Lara aside. He ran to Kate, who had halted several paces away and was staring, wide-eyed, at Lara.

"Hey! Where are you going?" Lara bleated, her cheeks puffy from crying. "You'll put your arm around me when your girlfriend's not around—why don't you just do it right in front of her?"

Kate gasped. Jake took her arm, but she thrust it aside and stepped forward toward Lara. "I can't believe this. What is going on?" She looked wildly from one face to the other. "Jake, tell me this is *not* happening." Her voice quavered. Jake prayed Kate didn't start to cry; he knew that if she did, Lara would move in for a quick kill. If Lara could be counted on for anything, it was a good fight. He had to get Kate away from her.

"Kate, look, let's get out of here. I'm sorry. The situation isn't what you think it is. Lara's just left rehab, and she's very upset—"

"Upset? I'm not the only one. Jake here was just

telling me how needy and moody you are, Kate—I guess *he's* pretty upset about that," Lara drawled nastily.

"What?" Kate's mouth dropped.

"You vicious bitch! Get away from me and my girlfriend. C'mon, Kate, *c'mon.*" Jake picked her up and dragged her toward the parking lot.

"Scared, Jake? Scared I'm gonna hurt your wimpy, prissy girlfriend?"

Kate tore loose from Jake's grip and wheeled around. "You *are* crazy! Why don't you just leave Jake and me alone! You belong in a *real* institution, not just a rehab center for alcoholics!"

Lara spat at Kate in response and ran to a silver Honda parked by the curb. She jumped in and drove off.

"Jake, oh, my God, that's the car your dad was talking about! The one tailgating him! I ran into him in Weymouth doing errands, and he told me he'd been tailgated by someone in a silver Honda—oh, Jake, when is this going to end?"

Jake dropped his face in his hands and groaned. When would it end?

The phone rang in someone grab that?" Darla bites of grapefruit. "Zo, Ben, eating!"

"Let the machine get it," growled Benjamin from the front hall, where he was packing up his surfer gear.

"You guys, God, it could be Lucas!" Zoey tore into the kitchen and lunged for the phone. She got it just as the machine picked up.

"Hello? Oh, wait, hold on a sec—lemme turn the machine off." She fumbled with the answering machine, cupping one hand to her mouth and saying, "Mom, I think it might be for Dad. It sounds like that accountant guy."

"Oh, no. I'll take it." Darla Passmore got up heavily from her chair. She held her hand out for the receiver. The answering machine still recorded, apparently not shut off correctly, and a man's voice blared, "Hello? Hello?" into the tranquil kitchen. "Is this Zoey Passmore? May I speak to Zoey Passmore?"

"What? Excuse me? Yes, this is Zoey Passmore." Zoey shook her head at her mom, who rolled her eyes and sat back down to her grapefruit.

attend a conference in _____, for outstanding student journal-_____ were one of over fifty nominees statewide _____ dered for the honor by a committee of five, including myself and your school newspaper adviser, and I am very pleased to congratulate you as our chosen representative to Washington."

"Are you serious? Me?" Zoey sat down, as if the weight of the news were too much to bear. Her mother clapped her hand to her mouth and began jumping up and down. "Benjamin," she hissed, "get over here! Did you hear what the guy just told Zoey?"

Benjamin crowded around Zoey excitedly. He held his thumbs up and waved his arms over his head.

"So, Zoey, your adviser will be calling soon to inform you of the details. Meanwhile I wanted to call personally and congratulate you. You're quite a kid."

The minute a dazed Zoey put down the phone her mother and brother broke into ecstatic whooping. "Zoey, this is amazing! Did you know you were nominated? Do you realize that was the head of the Weymouth paper? I always liked his editorials when Nina read them to me." Benjamin hugged his sister.

"I'm saving this tape forever!" cried Darla, holding up the answering machine. "Oh, I'm so proud of my genius writer daughter."

"Okay, Mom, you're laying it on a bit thick." But Zoey herself was starting to cry.

"We've got to call Jeff, guys." Darla dialed the restaurant. She pressed play on the machine when he answered, and they all listened again to the conversation. They could hear Jeff Passmore's voice squawking through the receiver.

"Honey, can you believe it?" Darla cried. "Zoey's going to Washington! . . . Yes, he just called. . . . Yes, Zoey didn't turn the machine off. . . . What? . . . Okay . . . okay . . . great, I'll tell her." Darla hung up the phone. "Zoey, your dad wants to throw a party for you at the restaurant. I'm going to run down there and help him get ready—why don't you two call up your gang and invite them?"

"Benjamin, will you call?" Zoey begged. "I just need to go to my room and let this sink in a little."

Benjamin cocked his head and scrutinized her. "That's very uncharacteristic of you. I'm the one who goes off to his room to mull things over while you call everyone you know and gossip your head off."

"I know, I know," Zoey concurred. "Just this once?"

"Sure, it's no problem, girl reporter. I'll rouse the forces." He mock-saluted her.

Zoey climbed the stairs to her room slowly and flopped down on her bed. She took out her journal. It seemed the only appropriate way to respond to an overwhelming jumble of feelings.

First of all, I can't believe Ms. Dodge nominated me as an outstanding student journalist; I thought she hated me! She's always telling me to cut, cut, cut... to keep my feelings out of the story... to stop using "pesky" adjectives that clutter up my prose. She's so prim and reserved. What's she going to say after I throw my arms around her and weep with gratitude!

Second of all, I can't believe I won! My whole life is beginning. (In a way it makes up for getting rejected by Stanford— I'd rather be singled out and honored for my writing, than "just make the cut" with SAT scores and math grades.)

But underneath all the

joy I feel something else.
Normally I would have
run to the phone and
called Lucas to tell him
the good news. But I
didn't. I told Benjamin
to phone my friends and
I retreated to the privacy
of my room. The truth is,
I'm kind of afraid to tell
Lucas. Not only because
he'll be sad I'm going
away to Washington but
because he might distance
himself even more from me.
Lucas feels like I'm leaving him behind, and in
more than one way. I
wish he could be happy
for me, but when his
alarm wakes him up at
five a.m. to drag in the
lobster pots, I doubt
what he'll be feeling is
happiness for me.

"Zoey, your fans are on their way!" Benjamin shouted upstairs. "What are you doing, writing your acceptance speech?"

Zoey's pen hovered over the page. She looked out the window at the Cabrals' house and then at the wall where she'd framed her first published article. "I'll be down in a sec—did you call Lucas, Benjamin?"

"Zo, are you kidding? Haven't you already called?" Zoey could hear the note of incredulity in his voice. She fidgeted with her hair, brushing it out of her face. Benjamin appeared at the door, slightly out of breath from taking the stairs two at a time. "Do you want me to call him?" His eyes narrowed wisely. "Hey, little sis—I think it's best if you do it, but if you aren't ready, I'll call. Okay?"

At times like these Zoey was grateful for having a brother like Benjamin. He understood, without her having to say a thing. She smiled, a little sadly, and whispered, "Okay."

Benjamin nodded and went downstairs. Zoey yanked her closet doors open and inspected the mish-mash of clothes accumulating on the floor. What could she wear? If she were Claire, she'd sport a scene stealer to ensure the proper attention. Claire was the type who'd try and upstage the bride at every wedding she attended. Aisha would wear a subdued and sensible ensemble to suit the respectability of the award. Nina—well, Nina might dye her hair a special pink for the occasion. Zoey smiled. Luckily the state of her closet made picking out an outfit relatively easy. She slipped the one clean blouse over her head and stepped into a long linen skirt. She gave herself a once-over in the mirror. Well, not exactly Kate Moss, but . . . it would do. It had to do because Benjamin was now waiting by the door.

When Zoey and Benjamin finally arrived at the restaurant, a sizable crowd of friends greeted them. Their parents had cleverly delayed their arrival by assigning a series of petty errands. Unfortunately one of these errands included picking up a pint of Ben & Jerry's ice cream, which by the time they arrived melted and seeped onto Zoey's tan linen skirt. Zoey laughed at herself. *I guess that's the Zoey Passmore fashion statement: Arrive at a party in your honor in a nice skirt stained with chocolate ice cream.* She brushed her long hair and applied lip gloss on the way into the restaurant. It seemed only minutes ago that she'd received the phone call, and now her parents were throwing her a spontaneous party: It was all a bit surreal. Her heart pounded as Benjamin held the door for her. How would Lucas react?

"Yippeeee! Zoey! Yeaaaah! Surprise!" A barrage of whoops, shouts, and catcalls (Nina's voice, of course) filled the room. Zoey blushed with pleasure and buried her face in her hands. It was practically more than she could take. Nina, Aaron, and Claire stood with their parents, drinking champagne in one corner of the room, while Aisha and Jake, along with their families, were interspersed among the tables. Aisha hung on Christopher's arm, beaming, her other arm swung casually over Kendra's shoulders. Zoey felt tears rush to her eyes.

"Congrats, Zo. I always knew you were our next Barbara Walters!" Mr. McRoyan shook Zoey's hand.

"Barbara Walters." Nina snickered. "Try Joan Didion! Or Danielle Steele? Danielle Didion? Argh, whatever . . . Zoey, I love you so much, and I'm so proud of you." Nina hugged her.

"Zoey, you're a good writer. You deserve this award." Claire's face looked radiant next to her pale blue angora sweater. She threw Zoey a brilliant smile and then snuggled into her perch on Aaron's arm.

Holding his champagne glass high, Jeff Passmore interrupted the festivities with a call for a toast.

"Dad, no. The last time you toasted Zoey at her sixteenth birthday party, half the guests fell asleep."

Everybody laughed, and Jeff made a mock angry face at Benjamin.

"Nonetheless, my son's complaints aside, I'm going to make you all suffer through a toast to my daughter. I'll make this one brief, I promise. First of all, I want to thank everyone for coming here on such short notice. But I know you're all looking for an excuse to party, anyway." Everyone broke into peals of laughter.

Zoey barely heard her father. She was searching the room for Lucas. The Cabrals' absence wasn't a surprise, but where was Lucas? She spotted Kate squeezed into a booth next to Jake. Kate sensed Zoey watching her and gave her a congratulatory grin. Zoey mouthed, "Where's Lucas?" and held up her hands in a gesture of puzzlement. Kate frowned, confused, and shook her head.

". . . Zoey, I'm proud to say, has been chosen out of the whole state of Maine to attend a conference in Washington, D.C., of outstanding student journalists. Our very own *Weymouth Times* editor—no comments from the peanut gallery, please—I myself don't always relish his editorials—called Zoey today to personally inform her of the honor. Of course, Zoey thought it was my accountant, calling to tell me Passmores' Restaurant ought to go public on the New York stock exchange."

Benjamin groaned. "Is heckling allowed?" he cried out sardonically.

"Okay, okay . . ." Jeff Passmore exchanged grins and quips with Aisha's parents, who, being small-business owners on the island themselves, best appreciated the joke.

Zoey threaded through the crowd to Benjamin. "Where's Lucas?" She took a small sip of her champagne. Benjamin scolded her.

"You're supposed to wait for your toast, dummy. He said he had to work. Didn't I tell you?"

"Oh." Zoey's heart sank. Working? How could she enjoy the evening when she'd just realized that the one person she truly wanted to be here was working? She tried to pull herself together for the benefit of her father, who was now addressing her.

"Zoey, you've always been a scribbler. In second grade your teacher, Mrs. Adams, took me aside and . . ."

Zoey's eyes glazed over. Her father adored telling the story of Mrs. Adams singling her out as a future "writer." It was so embarrassing.

"Hey, you look terrible," Nina whispered, slipping an arm around her. "Is it Lucas? Listen, I think he's being a jerk, too. Boycotting your party because he's too depressed to go? Lame."

Zoey stiffened. She gripped Nina's arm. "Nina, what did Lucas say? I mean, I thought he was working, and . . . and . . ."

Nina nudged her and jerked her chin toward Zoey's father, who was concluding his speech.

". . . Zoey, you make me proud to be your father *every* day, not just today. And if you write up our family secrets in the *National Enquirer,* heck, I'll be proud to see your name in print. Zoey, here's to you, and here's to Washington!"

The room burst out in applause. Zoey hid her face

behind her raised champagne glass. "Nina—tell—me—where—Lucas—is," she demanded between clenched teeth and a fixed smile.

"He's at home, you know, wallowing," Nina replied in a stage whisper.

Everyone clapped madly, looking at Zoey. "Speech, speech . . . ," Aisha and Christopher chanted in unison.

Zoey clutched her crumpled napkin fiercely in one hand. "Uh, gee, guys, thanks . . . what can I say?"

Eleven

Lucas breathed a sigh of relief. Docking his dad's boat in the Weymouth harbor always gave him the jitters. The general confusion of the dock—boats landing, men yelling, workers dragging tarps and tangled nets—distracted him from the delicate task at hand, which involved navigating the boat in parallel to a spot on the dock where he could toss a line over a free post. Lucas would sooner run away than face his father's wrath if he so much as scratched the old fishing boat.

After ensuring the boat was secure, Lucas hurried off to the fitness gym to find Zoey. At first he'd been discouraged by the fact that she was working all day, and he'd almost decided against his plan, but he figured if he timed it right, he could catch her on her lunch break.

And he had to see her alone. He had to tell her he was sorry, truly sorry. For hours last night he'd lain awake in his bed, kicking himself for missing her party. He'd even gone to the restaurant and lingered outside, trying to muster up the courage to go in. He'd watched through the window as Mr. Passmore toasted Zoey, he'd listened as practically everyone he knew and loved cheered her on. It brought tears to his eyes. But he couldn't bring himself to open the door. What would her friends and parents think if he strolled into her party two hours late? And he couldn't bear facing Zoey after he'd lied to Benjamin.

It was the phone call from Benjamin that did it. Lucas was so overwhelmed with the news of Zoey's latest, and greatest, success, he'd been speechless. The call came at the very worst moment: His father had just requested to speak with him in private. Lucas figured the worst and was hardly in the mood to hear about someone else's success, anyway. He'd freaked and impulsively told Benjamin he couldn't attend the party. Moments later Nina called, and he told her the truth: He was simply too depressed to face Zoey. He'd ruin the party for her. That was that. Looking back on the two phone calls, he wondered why it was so easy to tell Nina the truth.

An hour after the phone calls Lucas regretted his childish decision. The news from his father was actually good. Mr. Cabral's health had improved sufficiently, he felt, to go back to work. This meant that Lucas was free to enjoy the summer, provided he find part-time work to generate some income.

For Lucas it really only meant one thing: more time for Zoey. This was what he was striding through the streets of Weymouth to tell her. He fished in the pocket of his Windbreaker and felt the soft tissue wrapping of the present he'd made. Thank God, it hadn't fallen out. He grinned sheepishly. After acting like the world's biggest cad, the least he could do was bring a present, a gesture of apology. He hoped she wouldn't find it too hokey. He patted his pocket again.

A flower store display stopped him in his tracks.

Should he get her flowers? He bent down and inhaled a bunch of purple blossoms.

"Those are heather. They don't have much of a bouquet. Try these instead." Lucas jumped, embarrassed. A tall saleswoman stood over him, holding out a bunch of lighter purple flowers.

"Ummm, lilacs, huh?" Lucas inhaled deeply. They reminded him of the floral perfume Zoey wore on special occasions.

"Something for your girlfriend?" the saleswoman asked loudly.

"Uhhh, sorta . . . ," Lucas mumbled, panicking suddenly. All the different flowers in their colorful arrangements overwhelmed him. He didn't want to hand Zoey a prepicked bouquet of fancy flowers. It didn't feel right.

"Why don't you try a dozen of these lovely roses? Or we have a marvelous orchid selection. Orchids are such a *special* gift." Lucas disliked the way the woman emphasized *special.* He shook his head.

"Um, thanks, but I think I . . . uh—wait!" Lucas spotted the perfect thing. He pointed. "I'll take that, please."

"Potted pansies?" The woman looked at Lucas in dismay.

Lucas nodded.

The woman shrugged and rang up the purchase. She held the tiny pot of pansies as though it were a recently discovered carnivorous plant from the Amazon.

But Lucas knew it was perfect. Zoey would love the delicate flowers. He rushed to the gym, his heart thrashing with anticipation. What would she say when she saw him? Would she like his gift? Would she forgive him?

But when he arrived at the gym, his heart sank. Zoey wasn't behind the reception desk. The tall brunette in her place looked at him, eyebrows raised.

"Are you looking for Zoey? She just left for lunch. She always goes to Smoky Joe's lunch stand around the corner. You can probably catch her there."

Lucas thanked her and sprinted around the corner, clutching the pot of pansies carefully before him. He arrived just in time: Zoey was digging into her purse for money to pay the man behind the counter.

"I'll take care of that," Lucas offered, handing the man a twenty.

"Lucas?" Zoey's mouth dropped. "What are you doing here?"

"Taking you out for lunch. Should we go sit in the park?" He bent down and gave her a long kiss. He could smell a faint remnant of perfume mixed with sweet sweat, and it made him sad. She'd probably put it on last night, expecting to see him. Before she could ask any questions, he leaned forward and murmured, "Zo, I came to apologize. For everything, the—"

She clapped a hand around his mouth. "Don't. I know, Lucas. It's okay. It means so much that you're here. . . ." Her voice trailed off. She squeezed his hand. Lucas cleared his throat, conscious of people watching them. He felt like he had to stifle a sob. Zoey's capacity for forgiveness astounded him.

"But you know, Lucas, you still have to give me a huge present before you're fully off the hook. Like, say, a convertible."

"No prob, Zoey. A Thunderbird, red, 1966? It's on the way." Lucas smiled.

They sat down on a bench in the park, and Lucas

helped Zoey eat her fries. He himself was too nervous to be that hungry. He gave her the pot of pansies.

"Lucas! But it'll die when I go to Washington. I can hardly count on Benjamin to water it."

"Well, that's kinda why I got it. It's an excuse for me to go to your room every few days while you're gone. You know, so I can soak up enough Zoey particles to survive the week without you."

Zoey laughed. "What will *I* do? Eat fish all week long?"

Lucas brightened at the mention of his job. "Zo—my dad's going back to work. He won't need me anymore. I'm free!"

Zoey gasped. "Are you for real? You're not playing a joke on me?"

"Oh, yeah, right, some joke." Lucas rolled his eyes.

"Lucas, that's the best news I've heard all summer!"

He laughed at her, running his hand across her cheek. "Better than your journalism conference? Did I tell you how pretty you looked last night, even with the chocolate stain?"

She drew in her breath sharply.

"I stood outside, watching. But I couldn't get up my nerve to go in late. Here. Open it." He slid the package from his pocket and dropped it on her lap.

"Ohhh, Lucas . . ." Zoey bit her lip and looked at him softly. "I can't believe you were watching. If only I'd known. . . ." She fumbled with the tissue, stopping several times to look up at him.

"C'mon," he urged. She tore the last of the wrapper aside.

It was a shell. Lucas had found it on the rocky beach a few weeks past. Zoey turned it over. On the inside Lucas had glued a small black-and-white picture of the two of them. Kate had taken it that spring, one warm evening when they'd all hung out late at the beach. Both Lucas and Zoey were looking away from the camera. Zoey looked out at the water, and Lucas watched her. They were caught off guard, as if sharing secret poignant thoughts.

Beneath the picture he'd put something else. In careful black letters he'd written out his mother's recipe for sticky buns. Then he'd drawn one tiny, beautiful, black heart.

Twelve

"Nina, your handwriting is so messy on paper, how am I supposed to decipher it in the sand?" Benjamin fell to his knees and traced the indent of what was supposed to be a letter. "Is it an *E?* What happens if I can't figure out a letter?"

"Then you will never know the intensely sexy, passionate, and romantic message that I've created for you, my darlinck Benjamin. You will spend the rest of your life wondering . . . what was that message in the sand? Ahh, tragic young love." Nina practically had to yell because she lay next to the last letter of the last word of the entire message, which seemed to stretch halfway down the beach, or so Benjamin thought despairingly as he sat there stuck on the first word.

He'd been happy to see Nina. Between the disastrous night of the carnival and the party for Zoey he'd hardly gotten a chance to say a word to her privately. So when he emerged, exhausted, from the water to find her waiting for him, his heart leaped with joy. It was obvious that Nina was up to her old antics. She was theatrically posed next to her message in the sand, wearing a bikini, sunglasses, and a pink boa. Benjamin was immediately relieved; lately she'd grown increasingly morose and resentful, and for a second he worried she'd come to the beach to castigate him for surfing all day. But no—Nina had some mysterious tricks up her sleeve, and she was brimming over with enthusiasm about it.

"Where did you find that boa? In the attic?" Benjamin yelled.

"Ahh . . . monsieur, you are so crude. You cannot ask a woman to reveal her secrets," Nina replied, clearly enjoying herself. "But I will tell you this: It is an *E*."

"What is?" The wind almost drowned out his voice.

"The letter, stupid."

"Oh. Yeah. Okay, so what is this word—*booger?* Are you trying to tell me I have a booger hanging out my nose? Thanks for the publicity, Nina. You might have whispered it."

Nina collapsed in the sand, laughing. "*Booger.* Ha, ha. Are you losing your sight again? Try again. That's a *Y*, not an *R*."

Benjamin flinched at Nina's tactless joke. He decided to let it go. "Okay, let's see . . . *Y. Bogey?* Is that it? A nonsense word. Oh, wait a minute . . . Bogey as in Bogart? Humphrey?"

"Yes!" Nina jumped up and down, clapping. She imitated a sports announcer's voice: "It's one in the bag for Passmore. What a play. Score."

Benjamin bowed to an invisible crowd.

"Well, maybe it'll be easier now that I've got the general drift." He stepped back a few paces and surveyed the entire message. "Bogey—a *s-u-r-p-r-i-s-e,* okay, *surprise.* Then is that next word *awaits?* 'Bogey, a surprise awaits you' I assume that's me '*a-t s-u-n-s-e-t.*' *Sunset.* Okay, let me put it all together: 'Bogey, a surprise awaits you at sunset. Bacall.'" He looked up at Nina and grinned. "Well. My dear Bacall, of course *you* wouldn't be seen on the beach without a pink boa. I should have known."

Nina fluttered her eyelashes exaggeratedly in response. She could barely contain her giggles.

"Wait a minute, what's my surprise? It's almost sunset, isn't it?" Benjamin had a fleeting vision of him and Nina disappearing into the sunset on a Jet Ski. A couple of surfers told him it was the next-best thing to surfing the big, Hawaiian-style waves.

"Can't I have a little hint, my dear Lauren?"

Nina thought for a moment. "Well, our big date isn't tonight, Benjamin. I've planned it for tomorrow so you can go crazy with anticipation. And I most certainly won't tell you what it is."

"Nina, you can't keep secrets. All I have to do is tickle you in the right place and you'll tell me in ten seconds flat."

"Try me, Mr. Know-it-all." She crossed her arms and pouted. Benjamin paused dramatically and then threw up his hands. "Give me a hint, Nina. Are we eloping to Hawaii?"

"More like Paris, or a certain city in Morocco. That's a big hint." She pretended to draw a long drag on a cigarette. "That's another hint. But you have to imagine me with a pearl-inlaid cigarette holder. I'm blowing smoke rings that drift lazily over my bare shoulder. I don't talk much. And when I do, I drop suggestive one-liners in a husky voice."

Benjamin nodded, one eyebrow raised ironically. "So you're Lauren Bacall. I don't get it. Are we going to a costume party?" Meeting new people would be interesting, he mused. His old method of summing a person up—listening, feeling, intuiting— no longer suited him; now he could gaze at a person's face, amazed by the range of expressions each contained.

"I'd better try a different tactic. You're not even warm." She stared into space. "I'm searching for theatrical inspiration . . . hmmm . . . aha! Ready for an elaborate pantomime?"

Benjamin nodded. Since when was Nina so into parlor games? He wondered how long their little game would take and hoped he'd have time for one more spin in the water.

Nina pretended to chase an imaginary creature up and down the beach. She yelled to Benjamin over her shoulder.

"Okay, now I'm someone else. I have huge cheekbones and I wear men's shirts and right now I'm in a movie with your favorite actor, Cary Grant. My pet escaped, and I'm running around a funky Connecticut farm, looking for it."

"If I guess this one, will you tell me what our date is?" Benjamin asked.

"You'll never guess it, so I guess it's safe to say okay."

"Katharine Hepburn in *Bringing Up Baby*?"

Nina stopped short. "Benjamin, you take all the fun out of it," she complained. "Sometimes you're too smart for your own good."

Benjamin felt a little guilty. Maybe he'd unconsciously put his own agenda into the game—and thus brought an end to it. But if Nina wanted to fritter away the afternoon guessing movie trivia, well, then, frankly he was *glad* to put an end to it.

"Movie marathon," Nina announced. "With the whole gang—Cary Grant, Katharine Hepburn, Joan Crawford, Humphrey Bogart . . ."

"What?" Benjamin frowned.

"Our date. What's wrong? Why do you look so puzzled? You guessed the movie, didn't you? I rented all our favorite classics, and I'm going to make special Nina Geiger popcorn and hot fudge sundaes. It'll be a blast." She beamed. "Do I get a huge hug or what?"

Benjamin swallowed. "Wow, Nina, hot fudge sundaes and everything? Will you still wear the pink boa?"

All his fantasies—admittedly they were silly—of him and Nina waterskiing, or surfing, or riding a Jet Ski all disappeared in a flash. *Movies, huh? I'm sick and tired of movies!* But he couldn't let Nina sense his disappointment. She'd tried so hard, and she was so excited.

Aaron checked his reflection in the rearview mirror of his car. He wondered what Claire would see behind his poker face. Aaron was the master of concealment, but then, so was Claire, and she could read anything into a neutral facial expression.

Not that he had anything to conceal tonight. After all, it had been a purely platonic date. Fun, yes, even flirtatious—but he'd behaved like a gentleman. Which wasn't the easiest thing to do, considering how enticing she'd been. Of course, Lindsay wasn't anything like Claire, and she wasn't anyone he'd consider going out with, but she'd be pretty fun to kiss. He could tell from the way she'd licked the crumbs off the edge of her bread. She obviously didn't lack confidence. He sighed. Time to face Claire.

As he expected, Claire was loitering around the front hallway.

"Gee, expecting someone?" he teased, taking off his coat. "I thought maybe you'd be hiding in the backseat of the car the whole night, you know, just to keep an eye on things."

Claire shot him a disgusted look. "Puh-leeze. What do you think this is—*Fatal Attraction*?"

Aaron smiled dryly. "Sometimes I worry *you* think it is." He went over and kissed her. She smelled great, freshly showered and perfumed. He buried his face in her long dark hair. She wore a totally sexy outfit, presumably to upstage all competition. Aaron's eyes took in the low-cut velvet leotard and matching velvet leggings.

"You look ravishing," he whispered, running a hand down her back.

A small, triumphant smile played on Claire's lips. "Trying to distract me, are you?" she purred. "I'd like to hear what happened tonight. Did she fall hopelessly in love? Put her hand on your knee under the table? Did that picture of me I snuck into your wallet fall out at a strategic moment?"

Aaron took his hand away. He could tell he was in for a long, annoying night. He pursed his lips. "Claire, it was fine, okay? I did it for you. It was perfectly pleasant, it's over, I'm never going to see her again. Satisfied? And what was that about my wallet?"

He stared defiantly into Claire's eyes. He knew the more insulted he acted, the less guilty he would seem. On second thought, this only worked with less sophisticated girls than Claire, but it was too late.

She smirked. "Getting a little defensive, Aaron, aren't you? I mean, no need to put on the whole offended act for me. I know you. Do you find her attractive? Is that it?"

Aaron shrugged. "Sure, she's pretty. So what?" His voice was cold and remote. Why wouldn't Claire give

108

it up? She was making herself look so ridiculous. He loathed jealous, suspicious girls. Yet it was only because Claire knew his flirtatious, wily style so well that she guessed there was something to suspect. Claire, Aaron sighed to himself, would always guess correctly.

"All right, all right." Claire took his hand. "Forget it. Wait till you see what I've been doing all night." So she *was* giving it up. He breathed a sigh of relief.

Claire led him upstairs to her room. She shut the door with a conspiratorial air and then gestured to the bed.

On the bed was a minuscule tape recorder, headphones, and a tape. Aaron felt a thrill of excitement run up his spine. As a young boy he'd loved spy movies, and he often daydreamed about becoming a double agent or undercover reporter. Claire's elaborate schemes were the perfect outlet for his childhood fantasies.

"What on earth are you up to?" Aaron picked up the tape. "Isn't this an answering machine tape? Are you tape recording conversations or something?"

"Bingo," hissed Claire excitedly. "Do you remember how I was doing work for Daddy taping client requests? Well, Daddy has this cool equipment where you can record the phone conversations. That retard I went out with has been calling and leaving the most ridiculous messages, so I decided to have a little fun with him."

"Oh, my God. Claire, are you really that awful?" Aaron flashed her a wicked smile. *This* was the Claire he loved.

"Listen." Claire held up the tiny tape recorder and pressed play. Static crackled, and then Aaron heard a whiny boy's voice. Aaron laughed at the voice alone.

"Wow, what a drip. He sounds like a kid I knew who got beat up in fourth grade."

"Shhh . . ." Claire held a cautioning finger up to her mouth. "Listen."

"—and I just wanted to apologize for my disgusting, terrible behavior. You must hate me now."

"I don't hate you, Steven." Claire's voice, sultry and provocative. Aaron smothered a laugh.

"You don't?" The voice was uncertain now, faltering. "You're so sexy, Claire. I just couldn't help grabbing you like that."

"Have you thought about me a lot, Steven?" Aaron shook his head; he had a feeling he knew what Claire was up to.

"Oh, yes." There was a pause. "I've thought about seeing you again."

"Would you like to kiss me again, Steven?" Claire's voice, though calm and reassuring, was spellbindingly sexy.

"Oh, Claire, I'd love to kiss you, and hug you—"

"And what else?" Very deliberate, very quiet.

Another pause. "Can't say it?" Claire asked, her voice as sweet as honey. "Well, that's okay because you can't do it, either. But I'll be sure to let my boyfriend know—maybe he can get ideas from you!" Her voice broke into harsh, nasty laughter—then the phone clicked and static resumed.

"You hung up on him? Oh, wow, that guy will need years of therapy to get over you! You are so evil!" They both dissolved on the bed in a fit of hysterical giggles, which led to an impromptu make-out session.

Five minutes later the phone rang. Claire jumped up. "Aaron, what if it's him? Or his dad calling to tell my dad?" She looked at the phone in horror.

"Your deal. I'm not bailing you out of this. Pick it up." Aaron enjoyed seeing Claire frightened—she so rarely lost her cool. He lay back on the bed and put his hands behind his head. Cool, more entertainment.

"Hello?" Claire's voice was visibly agitated.

"Sorry?" She looked surprised. "Who? Uh . . . may I ask who's calling? Lindsay?"

Aaron bolted up. His first impulse was to grab the phone, but he exercised enough self-control to remain sitting on the bed. His heart dropped. Why was Lindsay calling?

Claire shot Aaron a poisonous look. "No, he's not here right now. This is his sister. Can I take a message?"

Aaron swore softly. He glowered at Claire.

"Uh-huh, uh-huh. Next Tuesday? And it's not called the Paper Mill Bar. Oh, I see. The Old Mill Bar. Yes, yes, I'll let him know. No, we certainly wouldn't want any mix-ups. Yeah. Thanks!" She put the phone back in the cradle.

"Never going to see her again, huh." Claire faced him and crossed her arms. She looked very pale. Her dark eyes sparkled with fury.

Aaron gulped. Now what he was he going to do?

Thirteen

Was the phone ringing? Kate turned over and buried her head beneath the pillow. She hated the sound of the phone's ring: It reminded her that life went on without her. The bustle of the world never stopped; it was just that she couldn't keep up with it. *The only thing in the world I truly love is my warm comforter,* she thought miserably. Even on a hot summer morning it was the only protection between her and the brutal world.

Even if the whole incident with her paper hadn't happened, even if she hadn't blown it with her favorite professor (and the one with the most potential influence on her career as an artist), well, she'd still be depressed.

First of all there was Lara. *I don't even want to think about her,* Kate thought, gritting her teeth. Growing up in New York hadn't exactly helped Kate overcome her fear of crazy people. *Isn't it ironic that I go to a place like Chatham Island, where no one even locks their doors at night, and I get stalked by a crazy person? Just my luck.*

She yawned. What time was it? Noon, Monday. She'd slept for thirteen hours. That was her response to depression: sleep. Sometimes she thought she could sleep for days on end. Was that the phone ringing again? God, it drove her crazy. Who could be calling? Surely not Jake. He was working. And hadn't Lucas mentioned he'd be off with Zoey all day? So it wasn't Zoey. Mr. Cabral woke up early to get to the boat, and Mrs. Cabral was most likely at church or shopping.

Kate rolled over. Whoever it was, she wasn't in any shape to deal with them. She felt almost resentful of any intrusion on her misery. She sniffed, feeling tears rush to her eyes. Then she opened them wide. What if the phone was Lara, or her mother, or school calling to say she was getting expelled for missing so many classes?

You're being paranoid, she told herself sternly. *Kate, snap out of it. Get up. Splash cold water on your face.* But she sank back down into the covers. *I'll just stay here an hour more. After all, I couldn't be paranoid when it comes to Lara. And I can't deal with that monster right now.*

Jake. Even the thought of him caused her grief. Although he'd denied it, he probably *had* complained to Lara about her neediness and depression. She could hardly fault him for it; who wouldn't be fed up with her? The situation had gotten out of hand. She *must* break up with Jake, even if it broke her heart. It wasn't fair to Jake to be saddled with a depressed, deadbeat girlfriend.

A tiny voice spoke in the back of Kate's mind. *You could always go back on the drugs.* Ugh. Drugs. Kate's mind roved back to the time over two years ago when, at the urging of her therapist, she'd gone on Prozac. At the time she was under incredible stress at the private school she attended. She was writing her final senior literature paper and finishing up a huge photography project. At some point she just couldn't work anymore. She gave up and slept all day and night. Her mother, frantic to help, begged her to go on Prozac.

It helped—Kate had to admit that the medication helped. She'd finished her paper and the photo project, though neither received the honors she'd expected. She'd stopped sleeping twelve hours a day and gone out more with friends. But her feelings about Prozac, and pharmaceuticals in general, were mixed. Kate didn't like the idea of putting drugs in her body on a daily basis—drugs whose long-term effects no one *really* knew.

Plus, deep down inside she sensed it dulled her creativity. It was hard to know this for sure, but she'd judged by the kind of pictures she took after going on Prozac. Although technically good and commercially quite viable—in particular she remembered a series of trendy shots taken of beautiful in-line skaters in Central Park—something was missing.

Her brain ached from too much thinking.

Please, whoever is up there, even though I'm not very religious, help me get out of bed.

In response, the phone rang. Kate sat up and looked at the extension by her bed. It rang seven times and then stopped. She sighed and stretched. It rang again. This time it didn't stop. In a fit of exasperation Kate reached out and grabbed it.

"What?" she barked, prepared for an onslaught of Lara McAvoy's spite.

"Mrs. Cabral?" It was a man's voice, breathing heavily as if he'd been running.

"Uh, no, she's not here right now. I'm her, uh, daughter, sorta. A family friend. Can I help you?"

"Miss, I'm Ben Caldwell with the Weymouth

114

police. I'm very sorry, but I have terrible news for you. Roy Cabral has suffered a very severe heart attack—"

"What?" Kate gasped.

"He's dead. I'm sorry, I know this is a huge shock. We tried to do everything we could, but he didn't even make it to the hospital. Can you tell me where to find his wife? We need her to come down to the hospital right away to identify the body."

"Identify the body . . . ," Kate murmured.

"I know, you're in terrible shock. I hate having to give you this awful news. I knew Roy myself."

Downstairs, a door slammed. Kate could no longer hear the policeman.

"I'll find her; we'll be there. The hospital in Weymouth?" She was surprised to find that she still had a voice.

"Yes, miss." He continued talking, but Kate dropped the phone into the receiver. It fell off and onto the floor with a bang.

"Kate?" It was Mrs. Cabral's voice. *She's coming up the stairs,* Kate thought with horror. *I have to tell her. Now. Nothing will ever be the same as it was a minute ago.*

"Are you still in bed? Get up, silly girl. Did school get canceled today or something?" Kate could hear her panting as she reached the top of the stairs. She stared at the bed, the comforter, her hand. *Mr. Cabral is dead. Dead.*

"Kate?" Mrs. Cabral stood at the foot of the bed, smiling, her face a picture of maternal concern. "Are you sick, honey? I made some blueberry muffins."

And then Kate was in her arms, sobbing. "I'm sorry, I'm sorry," she cried over and over.

"What did you do, honey? What are you sorry for?"

"Something happened to Mr. Cabral." Kate's voice was muffled by Mrs. Cabral's shoulder.

"What? Roy? My Roy?"

Kate stepped back and took a deep breath, trying to regain control of herself. "Mrs. Cabral, the police just called. They said he's dead. A heart attack."

Mrs. Cabral sat down slowly on the edge of Kate's bed. She frowned. "What are you talking about, Kate? Roy—my Roy? He's out on the boat. He's working." She didn't look at Kate but began slowly wringing her fingers around her dress. "He's working . . . ," she repeated mechanically.

Kate felt suddenly afraid. She bent down and took Mrs. Cabral's hand.

"The police just called and said he had a heart attack. They need you to go to the hospital. They need you to—to . . ." But she couldn't finish the sentence.

Mrs. Cabral's eyes clouded over. "My husband is working. There must be some mistake," she said, her voice loud and definite. She began rocking slowly back and forth, repeating the words to herself. "My husband is working. He's working. You know that, Kate. Don't joke with me. You know he's working."

Kate stared at Mrs. Cabral. Tears streamed down her face, but her eyes were blank and fixed on the wall. Her muttering grew softer. *Oh, my God, Mrs. Cabral is going crazy. She's in shock.* Kate realized she needed to be the one to take control of the situation.

"Mrs. Cabral, I'm going to call the police. They're going to come and take you to the hospital, all right?" She didn't take her eyes off Mrs. Cabral as she edged around the bed to the table. She dialed 911. Mrs. Cabral continued to rock back and forth. Her muttering grew more urgent. Kate wondered if she ought to accompany Mrs. Cabral or wait at the house for Lucas. Lucas. It was the first time she'd thought of him since the police called. Suddenly the full import of what happened reached her, and she could barely control the trembling in her voice.

"Hi, I need a police escort at 311 Climbing Way. Yes, I need to go to the hospital to identify a . . . a . . . a . . . body. What? They just called, yes. Yes, I received notification. When? Just now, I guess. No, no, I'm his friend. I'm here with his wife." Kate sobbed. "She's in shock. She needs someone to come out here and take her. Okay, yes, bye."

She hung up the phone. Thoughts raced through her head: Should she offer Mrs. Cabral something to drink? A stiff whiskey or water or what? Should she tell her again that he was dead? What was she supposed to do? Should she call her mother and have her talk to Mrs. Cabral?

Instinct took over. Kate sat down next to Mrs. Cabral and took her hand. She stroked it soothingly. Mrs. Cabral gave no indication she noticed Kate's presence. The two of them sat silently while the noise of a police siren, at first barely discernable, grew louder.

"Let's go downstairs and find your purse," Kate whispered. She stood up and led a dazed Mrs. Cabral down the stairs. "Careful, watch your step." She held Mrs. Cabral's hand tightly.

The policeman, assessing the situation instantly, took Mrs. Cabral's arm and steered her to the car. Kate grabbed the purse and house keys. *Who knows how long we'll be gone,* she thought. She dashed outside.

Mrs. Cabral was in the backseat of the car already. She leaned out the window and called to Kate.

"Kate?"

"Don't worry, I got your purse," Kate called.

"No . . . that's not it." The car started.

"Hey," Kate shouted. "Do you want me to come?"

"No." Mrs Cabral's face changed. "Find Lucas. Tell him that his father's dead. I can't do it, Katie. You go tell him."

The car eased out the driveway. Kate watched it until it disappeared, Mrs. Cabral's purse dangling from her arm.

Zoey spit bits of sand out of her mouth. "Lucas! You're getting sand in my mouth!" She pushed his lips away from hers. "Gross—where did you learn how to kiss, from a lobster?"

"My dad is a fisherman, Zo. Maybe I have sand for blood." Lucas rolled off her and brushed the sand off his face. They were lying in a sandy cove on the beach. It was the beach where they'd first kissed. Lucas had suggested spending the day here—the last day they had together before Zoey left for Washington.

Together they'd discovered a rock overhang. Two people could comfortably fit beneath it, at least horizontally. Zoey suspected this was the spot where Lucas hoped they would first have sex. She admired his ability to sustain the fantasy despite countless thwarted attempts. Still, she also sentimentalized the spot. How could she not? She'd spent some of the best times of her life wrapped in Lucas's arms here, listening to the waves lap the shore, and the gulls cry, and Lucas softly whispering in her ear.

"Are you excited?" Lucas asked, studying her face.

"Excited . . . about what?" Zoey picked a piece of sand from his eyelash.

"Going to the conference, silly."

"Oh, that. Of course. I'll get to meet all sorts of celebrities. Writers. Who knows? Maybe I'll shake Bill Clinton's hand."

Lucas laughed at her. "Romantic. You won't meet Bill Clinton."

Zoey sat up on one arm. "Why not?" she retorted, indignant. "Hillary's supposed to give the opening address. Who knows, maybe they'll have a reception afterward, and she'll mingle, and I'll happen to be standing—hey, are you listening to me?"

Lucas cocked his head to the beach. "Do you hear someone? Someone calling?"

Zoey listened. A gull squawked. Behind that, maybe . . . a girl's voice?

Lucas exhaled. "It's probably my mom looking for me. Or Nina looking for you. Let's ignore it." He kissed her cheek.

The voice was getting more distinct. It sounded like someone calling Lucas's name. Zoey wondered what it could be. She giggled and pushed Lucas away from her ear. "Don't lick it. That's gross."

"Hey! Since when do you find my kissing so gross? What if I pretend to be a celebrity journalist, huh? Then will you let me kiss your ear?"

"That's even grosser! Eeeuuuww. Bad." She swatted him and pulled him back on the sand with her. "Kiss me here." She pointed to the sunburn lines on her chest. "Softly."

"Ooooh. My pleasure." Lucas blew on her and then slowly lowered his mouth. Zoey wriggled in delight. His tongue ran delicately up and down her neck and chest. "Lucas, don't go down too far," she warned. His hands unfastened her bra. She sighed. "Oh, you're such a naughty boy, Lucas. *Lucas!*"

119

Suddenly Zoey heard another soft voice, a girl's voice. "Oh, God. I'm sorry, this is really embarrassing."

"Don't be embarrassed, Zoey. God, we're not doing anything," Lucas murmured.

"Lucas, that wasn't *me* talking." Zoey felt her face go scarlet. Someone was standing right there, looking at them, speaking to them. She couldn't bear to look.

"Ummm." Whoever it was hiccuped. Or was it a sob, Zoey wondered. Lucas had frozen.

"Lucas, I'm sorry, but I knew you'd gone to the beach with Zoey, and you showed me this special spot once, and I figured you'd be here. I just had to find you."

"Kate?" Lucas said, more as a statement than a question. "Is that you?"

Kate? Lucas had shown Kate their special spot? Zoey felt a wave of anger welling up in her chest.

"Yes, Lucas, it's me, Kate. I think you better come out."

"What's wrong, Kate?" Lucas slipped gracefully from under the rock. He reached back to give Zoey a hand. She fussed with her bra and fixed her shirt. Why was Kate acting so weird?

"I'm sorry, I'm sorry; I have to stop, I know." Kate held her hands over her face. Zoey realized suddenly that she was crying, desperately.

"Kate, jeez, don't feel bad, it's not such a big deal. Are you really that embarrassed?" Lucas shuffled his feet.

Zoey stared at Kate. She looked like she'd been crying for hours. Something was really wrong, something terrible. She took Lucas's arm. "Kate, my God, what happened?"

Kate turned to Zoey. "Lucas's dad. Dead. He's

dead. Lucas, your dad . . . a heart attack . . . oh, God, I'm sorry."

Zoey's fingers dug into Lucas's skin. Her mouth dropped. Time passed incredibly slowly, and all she was aware of was the sound of a gull screaming over her head. *That gull sure is loud,* she thought. *It's practically inside my head.* And then she realized it was she who was screaming, and the next thing she knew she sat on the sand, and Kate was hugging her, and she could taste her own tears.

Then Lucas was running toward the road, faster than she'd ever seen him run. "Lucas!" she called, but her voice was lost in the roar of the ocean. "Kate, stop Lucas, stop him. He'll hurt himself."

"No, Zoey," Kate answered softly, holding her. "Let him go. Let him go."

Fourteen

"Mr. Cabral? The nurse would like to see you and
your mother now."

Lucas started. He'd fallen asleep on his mom's
shoulder, except that he dreamed it was his father's
shoulder, and then the doctor called for his dad and
Lucas cried, begging him not to go. But it was he,
Lucas, they'd addressed as Mr. Cabral. Now he was
the caretaker of the family, the only man left. His
father was dead.

Lucas stood up and followed the nurse, his arm
around his exhausted mother. When he'd arrived at
the hospital, she was sedated. The nurse thought it
was advisable after her reaction to viewing her husband's body. To Lucas, his mother had become a
stranger: slurring her words, weeping profusely, and
even nodding off. But after the sedatives wore off,
she'd cried more hysterically, and the doctor was
reluctant to let her go home. He'd prescribed Valium
and given strict instructions to Lucas on how to best
care for her.

"Shock and bereavement are serious conditions.
Don't leave her alone, not even to take a bath. Hide
the medicine bottles from her. Make her hot drinks
and try to keep her in bed."

Lucas nodded to everything they told him. He hadn't shed a tear. He was too busy taking care of his mom.

Now the nurse handed him the prescriptions and directed them to the hospital exit.

"Do you need anything else?" Her face was caring and sympathetic. She patted Lucas's shoulder. "I'm so sorry." *I'll be hearing a lot of that from now on.* He felt like he was in a movie, some bad after-school special.

"Yeah," he muttered to the nurse in parting. *To hell with sorry. Where's my dad?*

At the exit an orderly met them with a package. "Sir?" He addressed Lucas. "Here are the clothes your father wore. You can take them with you now, or we'll send them, or we can destroy them. It's your choice."

Lucas took the package. *I'll bet it smells like fish.* The thought made him smile briefly. "Mom, we're going home. Okay? I love you, Mom." He put his arm around her protectively. Mrs. Cabral hadn't spoken for an hour.

A police escort took them home. Lucas slumped in the back, watching the lights of Weymouth slide past the window. Strange memories popped into his head. He remembered the year his father took him to Weymouth to pick out a Christmas tree. How old had he been—five, maybe six? He'd felt so proud when his dad let him pick out the tree all by himself. "If you pick it out, you have to carry it home on the ferry," his father had warned. And of course Lucas had picked out the biggest tree. And of course his father had helped him carry it. When they got home, his mom cried because it was the first Christmas they'd been able to afford real presents, and Mr. Cabral surprised her with the tree as an extra treat.

123

Lucas remembered walking down to the wharf with his dad. Everyone knew Mr. Cabral and liked him; he was a well-respected member of the fishing world. It had been a treat to walk the docks next to his father, listening to the men hail him and chuckle at his jokes. They always rustled up a present for Lucas—a lizard or a funny-shaped piece of drift-wood.

And then there was the time his dad helped him build the bookshelves. Lucas, an insolent sixth-grader at the time, insisted on using rotted wood he'd found in a junkyard. His dad only smiled faintly and encouraged him all the same. Together they diligently sanded and sawed and nailed together what Lucas considered to be the finest bookshelf ever built. Two weeks later, after it caved in on him, Lucas went sobbing to his father. "Why didn't you tell me rotted wood wouldn't work?" he'd demanded.

"You have to make your own mistakes and learn from them," his father replied. There was no doubt in Lucas's mind that in many ways his father had been a hard man. He'd never really forgiven Lucas for being sent to the Youth Authority, even after it became clear that Lucas was innocent. Lucas and his father had never had a chance to forgive each other for their mistakes.

Then Lucas remembered his father's boat. The boat. The *Lisboa* . . . Where was she now, without her sailor?

"Crazy driver, the light's red!" Nina gave the speeding motorist the finger. "Some people," she huffed.

It was the big night. Monday night. Hot and heavy date with Benjamin. Her knapsack weighed a million pounds from all the movies she'd rented. God, the bratty clerk even gave her a look, like, are you such a total nerd that you watch old black-and-white movies by yourself every night?

Nina couldn't stand meddling video store clerks. She squinted up the street ahead of her. Wasn't that hunched-over person weaving down the sidewalk Lucas Cabral? She waved.

"Lucas, hey. Yo, Cabral!" Sure enough. He looked up and then away. Weird. Nina stared in surprise as he crossed the street.

"Like, do I smell funny or what?" she shouted after him. Why would Lucas avoid her? Nina shrugged. This was ridiculous. In situations like this one, etiquette demanded that she run after him.

"Lucas, what's the scoop? Getting followed by the cops? Drug bust?" Nina gasped for breath as she caught up with him. The backpack was *really* heavy.

Lucas stopped and stared coldly at her. "Actually I'm going to the police."

His voice unnerved her. "Oh? I, uh, um, what for?" She couldn't help herself, though his tone warned her.

"To get the keys to my dad's boat. They have it locked up."

"Really? What happened—your dad get drunk and crash it?" She grinned at her own joke.

"No. He had a heart attack and died." It was said without a trace of emotion.

Nina felt her breathing jerk to a halt. She didn't say anything. She didn't bat an eyelash. Lucas continued to look at her stonily.

"Mind if I walk you there? To the police?" Nina asked finally. Her voice was quiet. Lucas hesitated, eyeing her suspiciously. He shrugged.

"Nope, I don't mind."

They walked together in silence. Nina thought: Roy Cabral died. It didn't surprise her, but then nothing like that would ever surprise her in the same way since her own mother had died. She didn't bother to second-guess Lucas. She didn't even wonder why he'd sprung it on her like that. In fact, she realized she felt oddly comfortable with him.

It was dusk, and a slight drizzle emptied the streets of people. Nina wondered if a summer storm was coming. Claire would know.

"Are you going to tie down the boat? What's the name of it, the *Lisboa*?"

"Yeah. I'm going to tie it down. Look, there it is," he said, pointing at a fishing boat moored next to a sleek Coast Guard motorboat. "The *Lisboa*. Lisbon. Funny, I've never even been to Portugal."

"Oh, yeah?" Nina walked, without knowing why, toward the boat. *But he has to get the keys. Where am I leading him?*

But Lucas followed her.

"I've been to Lisbon. Did I ever tell you that? I guess not—we never talk much about anything but Zoey. Anyway, it was a long time ago. Mom and Dad took us . . . shall we get on it?" Nina asked, gesturing with her eyes to the boat. She realized she had to get on first. Lucas needed her to get on first. She continued talking. "Well, they took us to the Algarve. That's a beach resort in the south, on the coast. It was nice, what I can remember." She helped Lucas over the side and sat down next to him in the stern. "Anyway, Lisbon was really, really cool. Claire and I played tag in the tiny, cobblestoned streets. And you wouldn't believe the harbor there. Huge fishing boats!"

Then Lucas was crying, silently. His body shook.

Nina put her arms around him, and he put his head in her lap. His chest heaved with sighs. Nina watched as her own tears dropped onto his T-shirt. Long ago she'd learned how to cry silently. But now she couldn't keep a sob from escaping.

Later, Nina touched Lucas's shoulder gently. They'd been sitting in silence for some time. "Lucas? I gotta go meet Benjamin. Do you want to come?"

Lucas shook his head. "No, I think I'll stay here for a while. Thanks. I think I'll just stay here."

Two hours later Nina knocked at the Passmores' front door. Benjamin hadn't shown up for their date. She figured he was here, at his house, comforting Zoey. Still, Nina couldn't help feeling an eentsy bit miffed that he hadn't called. After all, it wasn't his father who had died. She looked forward to receiving an explanation of sorts.

Mr. Passmore answered the door. His face was drawn and pale. "Have you heard the news, Nina?"

She nodded.

"Zoey's upstairs with her mom if you want to go up."

"Oh, actually I was looking for Benjamin. I mean, I want to see Zoey, but Benjamin was supposed to meet me at my house and he never showed."

"That's odd." Jeff Passmore looked perplexed. "He told me he was getting a painting lesson from Lara in Weymouth."

"Are you kidding me?" Nina's face darkened. "A painting lesson—in Weymouth?"

"He left over an hour ago. I just called over there, but I guess they're out for dinner. I'm sorry, Nina. Look, I wanna go back upstairs. Darla and I are talking to Zoey. She's pretty upset. C'mon in and help yourself to whatever." He disappeared down the hall-way.

Nina marched into Benjamin's room and turned on the light. Her first impulse was to toss all his precious CDs out the window. She grabbed one and threw it against the wall. The sound of the case snapping in two only made her angrier.

How could he? "Benjamin Passmore, you are turn-ing into one royal ass!" Nina shouted, tearing an upside-down poster off the wall. She didn't care if any-one heard her; how could anyone in the house get any *more* upset? "I hate you, I hate you, I hate you!" she chanted through gritted teeth. Who did he think he was, some kind of stud on *Baywatch*? The prince of Chatham Island? Nina threw herself on his bed and pounded her fists into the pillow.

Her fist hit something. It crackled. She sat up abruptly. A note. Written in neat, girly cursive, it read:

Dear Benjamin—I'm sorry we couldn't have a photography les-son this afternoon as we planned. Something urgent came up. I'll speak to you about it later. Please tell Zoey to wait until tomorrow to stop by.

Love, Kate.

Nina, take a deep breath and don't scream. . . .
Okay, okay, okay.

She read the note again. *Let me get this straight, Benjamin. You scheduled not one, but two other engagements during our Big Date? The date with Kate must have started at four. So you'd be, say, an hour late to my house. Except that you'd have to leave in five minutes to make the ferry to Weymouth. Bastard.*

It didn't help matters much that the girl signing the note was Kate. Nina's wounds had barely healed from the "Kate" episode. She flashed back to seeing Kate kissing Benjamin in this very room.

Did Benjamin no longer love her? Or was he a different Benjamin, a new Benjamin eager to discard his old habits, including his old Nina habit? It wasn't fair. Everything in this room reminded her of Benjamin: The clever Benjamin who hung his posters upside down and wore all black, the sophisticated Benjamin who appreciated Japanese noise bands *and* Beethoven, the sweet Benjamin who massaged her feet while she read aloud.

Am I nostalgic for someone who no longer exists?

Nina found a pen and smoothed out the note from Kate. It needed a few more words.

Zoey

I can't believe Mr. Cabral died. I can't believe this is happening in my life. I never thought I'd be consoling my seventeen-year-old boyfriend about his dad's death. I never thought I'd have to look Lucas in the eyes and tell him, "I'm sorry your father's dead." I know there's nothing I can say to him that will make him feel better, but I can't help trying. I just wish I could understand how he feels, but that's impossible. I know it's the kind of thing that you can't understand until it happens to you. But still, I want to do all the things

to Lucas that I imagine
I'd want someone to do
for me—like making him
brownies, washing his
clothes, getting him flowers,
and holding him at night
while he cries himself to
sleep. But Lucas doesn't
want any of this right
now. So what do I do?
Nothing? Just stand by
and watch while he suffers
what will be one of the
greatest losses of his life?
Write him a letter? Go and
try to comfort his mom? I
guess I feel like I have
to do something.

After all, I'm Lucas's
girlfriend. Isn't it my
responsibility to step in
and try to help the fam-
ily? I can't help feeling
hurt that Lucas rejects
every effort I try to make,
but maybe that's what he

needs to do right now.
Maybe before he can grieve
with me he has to grieve
privately by himself, and
the nicest thing I can do
is sit back and watch.

I think I'll go give my
dad a hug.

As for the conference, I
feel guilty even mentioning
it. I can't believe one of
the best and the worst
things that have ever happened to me happened in
the same week.

LUCAS

When Wade died, I remember thinking nothing like this will ever happen to me again. I remember watching Jake at the funeral and thinking, "I don't know how he could stand to lose his brother." For days people were really nice to Jake and then they stopped calling and coming around, afraid and at a loss for words. How many times can you say, I'm sorry? I thought nothing like that would ever happen to me.

Now I know better. It's weird. I expected my father to live forever. I took him for granted, and I never felt bad all those times I cursed him to myself and wished he wasn't my father. All those times

we fought about the fishing
boat or reform school, I
never thought I would ever
have to say I was sorry. Now
I wish I had the chance.
If only I'd been there on
that boat to hold his hand
while he went. If only he'd
known that I was with him
And that I loved him.

Fifteen

The phone rang just as Benjamin put a dab of paint on his finger. Lara offered the use of a small canvas, and she suggested starting out with a finger to "get to know the paint." They'd talked for nearly an hour about different aspects of painting and flipped through some of Lara's art books (shoplifted, she proudly informed him). Benjamin was anxious to start painting.

Now the phone rang. "Bummer," said Lara. She hurried to get it.

She hasn't been so terrible to hang around, Benjamin reflected as he studied his canvas. Not terrible at all. Of course, Zoey would throw a little fit if he said so. Merely *contacting* Lara was criminal in her book. But it was mutual. And Lara was kind of crazy, and vicious, and who knew what else . . . but hey, Benjamin reasoned, if they were all stuck with her, why not make the best of it?

Lara tapped him on the shoulder. "It's Dad. He wants to tell you something."

Benjamin could tell from the expression in her eyes that he'd already told her. *What kind of something,* he wondered. The last time he'd received an important phone call from his dad, Lara had run away from rehab. How much drama could one family take? That phone call was enough for him. He'd fallen asleep on Nina's couch, and . . . Nina? . . . Something stirred vaguely in the back of his mind. He took the phone.

"Dad?"

Jeff Passmore was curt. "Roy Cabral died. Come home now."

Benjamin felt a wave of relief. Thank God, nothing had happened to Zoey or his mom.

"Heavy, huh?" Lara put the phone back. "Just like that. Heart attack."

"Where was he when he died, did Dad say? Lucas and his mom weren't there, were they?"

"No. He was fishing. Boy, I guess the guy was sicker than he thought. Tough old man. That's the kinda guy you think is gonna last until he's a hundred and five."

Benjamin nodded. But Lara's flippancy repulsed him.

"Yeah, well, see ya later, Lara, okay?"

She pouted. "Going already? I'm so lonely these days—let's go bowling!"

Benjamin couldn't help flashing her a look of shock. Then he shook his head. In one quick dash he was out the door and down the street.

Arriving home, he found the house empty. The door to Zoey's room was closed. She'd probably gone to sleep. A note on the kitchen table left by his mom said they'd gone for a walk.

Benjamin grabbed a soda out of the fridge and wandered to his room. He didn't bother turning on a light; there wasn't anything in his room he cared to look at. He certainly didn't need a light to get around.

But the bed rustled when he lay down. He felt the

sheets beneath him with one hand, then turned on the light next to his bed. It was the note from Kate. He'd found it that afternoon. Now he understood why she'd had to cancel. Wasn't there something he should tell Zoey? He skimmed it quickly, and then some handwriting at the bottom caught his eye: It was Nina's.

P.S. Dear Benjamin, if only you'd had the decency to write me a note as nice as this canceling our Big Date. But I guess you forgot about it altogether. Call me when you think you can pencil me in between your many arts and crafts.
Hate, Nina.

Benjamin's head dropped into his hands. *Am I going crazy? How could I have really forgotten something so important? What is it that I really want?*

JAKE

Why do tragedies like this happen on our little island so much? Am I imagining it? Or does it seem like we get more than our share? I feel so sorry for Lucas. The day after Wade died, I went out in a little rowboat by myself. I rowed and went way out in the ocean. I think in a way I was hoping that a storm would come and that I would drown.

I felt guilty that it was Wade and not me that died. But no storm came. And I just sat there looking at the sea for hours. I didn't really think much of anything at all. But when I came home, I hugged mom and I felt better. I hope Lucas finds his own way.

Kate

Tomorrow's the funeral. I'm so
exhausted that I'm worried I'm
going to fall asleep during it.
All day long I was making
plane arrangements, calling relatives in Portugal, cleaning the
house, and helping Lucas get his
dad's stuff organized into boxes.
I never knew death required so
much work, so many details, so
many things people leave behind
when they go. I'm worried about
Mrs. Cabral, but in a way her
crazy grief is preferable to Lucas's
catatonic silence. I can tell he's
shut down and doesn't want any

one to try and help him. He yelled so hard when I dropped the TV, you'd think I dropped his dad's vintage bottle of port. I guess he needs something or someone to yell at. Oh, I'm so tired. And Mom's coming....

Sixteen

"Jake, Mrs. Cabral says you'll find Kate upstairs. Why don't you go on up." Mrs. McRoyan smiled anxiously. Jake could tell she was worried about Ilse Cabral. Mrs. Cabral had been there for her when Wade died—comforting, running errands, cooking— and now it was Mrs. McRoyan's turn to do the same. With the funeral the next day, there was a lot to be done. Clearly she wanted Jake out of the way.

Jake climbed the stairs with some trepidation. Did Kate want to see him? Would Mr. Cabral's death throw her into a deeper depression? Worst of all was his gnawing suspicion that Kate's depression had something to do with him. Surely he'd said something tactless to hurt her feelings or neglected to take them into account. And then the Lara incident. He'd really botched that up. Their relationship was under enough pressure without the enormous strain of Lara's theatrics.

"Jake?" Kate called. "Is that you?"

It was good to hear her voice. "May I come in?" he asked, his voice husky.

She opened the door. Despite the past day's events she looked fresh and vigorous. She wore a vintage black dress with a white lace collar. It looked ancient but well made. She caught Jake looking at it and smiled. "My grandmother's. I'm wearing it to the funeral."

Jake took her in his arms. "It's beautiful. So perfect for you."

"You're not supposed to admire funeral attire." Kate laughed jaggedly.

Jake glanced around the room. Photographs were spread all over the floor. A bottle of glue lay open on the desk. "I'm making a collage for Mrs. Cabral. Of all the pictures I've taken of Mr. Cabral," Kate explained. "It's the least I could do." She sighed.

"Kate, are you okay?" Jake asked seriously.

"Well, it's really a blow. I'm so close to this family, it's almost like losing a father. A father figure."

"Of course," Jake said politely. "But Kate, I mean, how are *you* doing," he persisted. "I know you cut classes yesterday, and you've seemed sad a lot recently. Have I done anything? Is it me, Kate?" His eyes pleaded with her.

"Oh, no, Jake, it's nothing to do with you at all! I mean, the whole Lara thing upsets me, but really i-i-it's not you. Oh, Jake, I, um—"

Jake stepped forward and took her hand. "What is it?"

"I want you to meet my mom," Kate finished weakly. "She's coming here today for the funeral."

"Oh," Jake said. "I hope she likes me."

"I'm sure she will." But Kate didn't sound at all sure.

Aisha

It's the middle of summer, and all of us are poised to leave Chatham Island to begin our separate adult lives. Boom. Lucas's dad dies. Our little world is shattered. When I first came to this island, I remember feeling like an outsider. How could I ever penetrate the inner circle of people who have grown up and spent their lives together on this island? Now I belong here as much as anyone else, and I realize how important community is to everyone on this island. Lucas's dad dying isn't just a blow to the family; it's a blow to all of us.

As I write this I can hear my mom downstairs crying quietly and talking with my dad. I'm sure my mom is thinking of Mrs Cabral and thanking God

that it wasn't my dad. The
funeral is tomorrow. What can I
possibly say to Lucas? Death is
the ultimate irrationality. Maybe
I'm just too young to understand. And Lucas is too young,
too, but he doesn't have the lux-
ury of growing up first.

Lara

Oh, my God. Lucas's dad died. I'm so tripped out. I wonder if I went too far that day at the carnival when I told everyone their fortunes. Little did I know a real disaster would happen. I feel kind of guilty like I worked some black magic without even realizing it.

Of course, I won't even be invited to the funeral. But Kate will, and Jake will be giving her all sorts of sympathy since she's Mrs. Cabral's little pet. I'm sure she didn't even like Mr. Cabral. He was a grouch. Of course, Lucas wouldn't admit it, but he always hated his dad.

One time I overheard him telling Jake he wished he'd had Jake's dad instead of his own. Boy he regrets saying that now.

And Zoey, she was terrified of Mr.
Cabral. She acted all sweet and fake
around him, but really she was shaking in
her shoes. My dad always used to talk
about Mr. Cabral's bad temper. No
wonder he had a heart attack. Well, I
didn't know Mr. Cabral, so I can't say
anything about him, but the rest of them
can rot in hell.

Christopher

Today Lucas's dad died. It's so weird; it was only a week ago that I went over there and Mr. Cabral caught us smoking a cigar on the front porch. He was always so mad at Lucas that I tried hard to make the blame fall on me. "Don't worry, Mr. Cabral," I said, "I smuggled them onto the island from Weymouth to smoke after our weekly poker game. For once Lucas didn't have anything to do with it. And besides, you know I'm going to be a successful businessman someday, and they always smoke cigars." Mr. Cabral thought that was funny and he laughed.

I think he always liked me because he knows how hard I work. Lucas's dad has the strongest work ethic of anyone I've ever met. If he worked on Wall Street, he'd be a billionaire. I guess Lucas never could appreciate that side of him because Mr. Cabral was always faulting him for not working hard enough. I wonder where my own father is. In a way, it would be easier for me if he were dead.

BENJAMIN

I've tried too hard to live to think
much about death. Though most of
my life has been spent in the dark,
it's nothing like the blackness I imagine to be death. Tomorrow is Roy
Cabral's funeral. It's strange to think
I've lived all my life next door to him.
How many times have we said hello?
Passed each other in the street?

I'll miss the smell of him: a combi-
nation of leather, wind, and salt.

Claire

Today Lucas Cabral's dad died. I went up to my widow's walk and sat for a long time looking at the cloudy sky, thinking of that day when Daddy told me that mom was dead. I was almost too little then to understand what was happening. I remember meeting Mr. Cabral for the first time a few months before the car accident. It seems like yesterday, but it was four years ago. Lucas was kissing me on the dock, and we heard someone clear their throat. We looked up, and I saw this little old man wearing funny suspenders holding a lobster pot.

Lucas was blushing like crazy, so I guessed it was someone in his family. His dad shook my hand like a gentleman and when Lucas wasn't looking gave me a wink.

It s been a long time since I've been close to Lucas, but I guess I still feel love for him. People think of me as cold and unsentimental, but I've never really stopped caring for any of my old boyfriends. And how could I stop caring for Lucas? So many things have happened since we went out.

I know he doesn't like me. But I wish there was some way that he could trust me enough to listen to me tell him all the things I've learned about dealing with the death of a parent. On second thought, what have I learned? Just that the pain never goes away.

Nina

I can barely stand sitting here inside the house, knowing Lucas is over there alone. I know exactly how he feels right now. It's strange, but the more I've gotten to know Lucas recently, the more I notice that we have a lot in common. Now we have a new bond, and it's a bond that cuts the closest to the bone.

I still miss Mom every day. I think probably Claire doesn't miss her as much as I do, but a day doesn't go by that I don't think about her smile or her smell or her voice. But Mom knew how much I loved her. I wonder if Lucas ever said those words to his father: "I love you."

It's weird that I feel such a strong urge to help Lucas. It's almost like I think I'm the only one who can. Maybe it's just that he's been confiding in me so much lately and avoiding Zoey. I love Zoey, and I think she's one of the most insightful people that I've ever met, but I don't think she could ever understand what he's going through right now.

Seventeen

Nina walked stiffly between Aaron and Claire into
the church. She hated funerals, especially the ridiculous clothes people wore to them. "But I thought
you loved black," Claire whined during breakfast.
"It's *your* fashion event." Luckily their father inter-
ceded for once and told Claire to keep her sick jokes
to herself. That hadn't stopped Claire from abusing
Nina the whole way to the church. Not in a pleasant
mood herself, Nina lashed back. "What happened,"
Nina retorted, "did you and Aaron get in a fight or
something? Need to take it out on your little sister?"
That had shut Claire up in a hurry. Her mouth
opened and shut quickly. Nina even detected a slight
blush.

Now Nina took the offensive. "You sit next to the
wicked step," she hissed to Claire. "I'm sure she'll
sing all the hymns in tune, and maybe she'll offer you
her hankie when you get weepie." Claire ignored her
and sat next to Aaron.

Nina was in such a hurry to reach the other side of
the pew before her father and Sarah arrived that she
didn't see Benjamin until she'd practically run
straight into him.

"Nina?" Benjamin said, surprised. "Are you running away from me? Nina, I'm sorry. I feel terrible."

"Don't condescend to apologize to me here, Benjamin," Nina snapped. "At least save the lies for outside the church. It's supposed to be holy, right?" She brushed past him and sat next to Aaron.

The processional music began. People had taken their places in the pews and were quieting down.

Nina met Zoey's eyes. Zoey had obviously overheard her exchange with Benjamin, and her face registered shock. She stared at Nina incredulously.

"Ask Benjamin, why don't you," Nina said curtly.

The people in the pew in front of them turned around to see who was being so rude. Nina grinned and pointed to herself.

"Oh, God, here she goes." Claire dropped her face in her hands. "Daddy, make Nina cut it out—she's insulting everyone," she whispered.

Burke shot a nasty glance at his daughters and shook his head in disgust. Sarah rummaged anxiously in her purse for a moment and then waved a bottle of Tylenol at Nina. "Do you want?" she mouthed, pointing at the bottle. This produced a fit of giggles in both girls. Aaron, stuck in the middle, flipped through a Bible and tried to appear oblivious.

The processional began. Nina's giggles stopped midway in her throat. The pallbearers, grunting from the strain of the coffin, carried it up the aisle. Nina's hand instinctively sought Claire's—and found it. She knew what Claire was thinking. *I can't look at her, or I'll start to cry.*

She looked. Claire's eyes rimmed over with tears. She swiftly crawled over Aaron and sat next to Nina, clutching her with both hands. "I know, I know," Nina whispered, smoothing her sister's hair. She squeezed her hand.

"Aaron thinks we're crazy," Claire murmured, sniffling. "Probably. It's not his fault." Nina darted a glance at Aaron and then her father. What was Burke thinking, sitting there next to his new wife? Was he remembering, too?

Mrs. Cabral walked down the aisle, veiled, with Lucas behind her. Nina craned her neck to see his face.

But all she saw was his tight, miserable shoulders. He sat next to his mother in the front pew.

The minister began with a passage from Genesis. "Ashes to ashes, dust to dust . . ."

But Nina's mind was wandering. She stared at the candles flickering above the casket. Why did people always put such dumb, fake-looking flowers on caskets? She remembered hating the flowers on her mother's casket. In fact, she remembered hating everything about the funeral. Her dad had organized it, and of course her uncle, who had later molested her, was there.

Someone blew their nose loudly. Nina stole a peek at her father. He stared straight ahead, but a telltale tissue lay on his lap. A cold? In June? No way. Burke Geiger was crying. As she watched, fascinated, a tear ran down his cheek.

Nina closed her eyes.

Zoey fixed her eyes on the back of Lucas's head. She didn't want to look at the ugly, gleaming casket on the altar. She tried putting herself in Lucas's place. What would she be thinking if her own father lay in a casket twenty feet away? She shivered.

She'd spoken to Lucas once since the fateful moment Kate found them making out on the beach. She called, and he picked up the phone. She asked if he wanted her to come over. "No," he'd replied sullenly.

Can I bring you or your mother anything? No. Are you doing all right? Yeah.

His icy silences and brusque tone got to her so much, she started to cry. "Lucas, please, talk to me. Let me help you, please. . . ."

But he'd told her curtly that she couldn't understand, that it was best for both of them if she left him alone. Then he hung up.

Zoey, no matter what her mother told her—"He's angry, dear; he'll get over it," or, "It's the first stage in a normal healing process"—felt woefully inadequate. Wasn't she the solid, loving girlfriend, ever ready to lend a helping hand? Maybe Lucas didn't think so.

She tried to catch his eye as he walked down the aisle, but he looked above the sea of faces staring at him. If he wouldn't even look at her, how was she supposed to talk to him? They *had* to talk. Soon. She ran through the conversation in her head.

Lucas, I'll cancel my trip to Washington if you think you need me even a little. Do you want me to stay with you? This was where the practice conversation always ended. Zoey was afraid of the answer. Either way she lost. If she stayed, she'd miss out on the best opportunity she ever had. If she went, she'd feel guilty forever. (And rejected?)

Her heart jumped: Lucas was walking to the podium. He adjusted the microphone and took a piece of paper out of his pocket. The room was utterly silent. Zoey struggled to maintain her composure. She didn't want to drown out Lucas's speech with her sniffles.

Lucas fumbled with his notes. He frowned. "I don't need these," he muttered, returning the handful of papers to his pocket.

"Everybody here knew my dad. I don't need to try and sum him up. I wouldn't want to if I could. How do you sum a person up when they die? 'Roy worked hard, he liked bacon for breakfast, he was good to his wife'? Even if all that's true, I don't know what it means. People say my dad was a simple man. Maybe in some ways he was. But that's not the person I'll remember." Lucas paused and gazed into the distance. For a moment Zoey was afraid he'd become so engrossed in memories, he'd forgotten where he was.

"My dad surprised me once. I woke up at dawn to hear him talking downstairs in the kitchen. I wondered who he was talking to. Nobody I know rose as early as my dad, not even the other fishermen. I crept downstairs, and there was my dad, talking to this little bird at the feeder in the window. He saw me spying, and he winked. 'Watch this, Lucas,' he whispered. He held out one finger and whistled softly, and sure enough, the bird came and perched on his finger. As soon as I moved closer, the bird flew away. My dad laughed and said I hadn't learned yet, hadn't learned how to be a bird. I thought he was crazy at the time, but now I think I understand." Lucas nodded to himself. He took a deep breath and looked around the church, then at the coffin.

"I'll miss my dad," he said simply, then left the podium.

Zoey sighed. Their eyes met. As Lucas sat down, he looked at her. For a second she thought she saw a wink.

Eighteen

The reception was held in the churchyard. Kate helped her mom carry food and drinks to picnic tables arranged in a semicircle in the back of the yard. They were in the middle of squabbling over how to arrange plates of food when Jake sidled up.

"Hi, Kate. I saw you carrying some pretty heavy trays over there. Do you need a hand?"

"Oh! Jake! Uh, this is my mom, uh, Mrs. Levin. Mom, this is Jake McRoyan." Kate was sure she sounded like a dope. Jake's sudden entrance had flustered her.

"Pleased to meet you." Mrs. Levin grasped Jake's hand and shook it very formally. "I hear you've been spending quite a bit of time with my daughter."

"Uh, yeah. Sure have." Jake made a painful attempt at a smile. Kate saw that he was sinking beneath her mother's cold scrutiny. She tried to interrupt. But she was too late.

"So, Jake, what kind of educational activities do you pursue?"

"Educational activities?" Jake stumbled over the word *educational*.

Mrs. Levin gave him a thin-lipped smile. "In other words, what else do you do other than football?"

Jake brightened. "Well, I'm doing a lot of A.A. You know, Alcoholics Anonymous? That's been very educational for me. It's a whole system of thought, I guess."

Kate blanched. A.A. had not been high on the agenda of things she wished to see her mother and Jake discuss. In fact, she'd prayed desperately it wouldn't come up at all.

Mrs. Levin glared at Jake through her gold-rimmed glasses. She cleared her throat briskly. "Kate, we must help unload the car. This way, please."

"Uh, can I help?" Jake asked, his face beet red. Kate awarded him an A for effort. At least he didn't give up and return the insults.

But Mrs. Levin pretended not to hear the offer. She hustled Kate off to a quiet corner of the yard. "What is this nonsense about A.A.? Why didn't you tell me the boy's an alcoholic? What's gotten into you, Kate?"

"Mom, you've been firing questions at me all day! Can you stop? Jake's had problems with alcohol, but he hasn't had a drink in months. Can't someone live down their mistakes? If you took the time to talk to him, you'd realize he's a nice person."

"Oh, God, where have I heard that before? Don't be naive, and don't think you can fool me. You're depressed again, aren't you?"

"Why do you say that?" Kate asked carefully.

"Ilse mentioned you've been staying home from school sick recently. I say, sick, what's the girl sick with? And Ilse shakes her head. Why she tries to protect you is beyond me. You're not sick, Kate. You're cutting classes and sleeping all day."

Kate looked at the ground. "So?"

"So? That's all you have to say? Speak for yourself, yell back, whatever, anything but this sullen 'so.'" Mrs. Levin gestured wildly.

Kate remained silent.

"Kate, I've come here to take you back to New York. You need to see your old doctor and go back on the medication. This is an order, not an opinion. Do you understand?"

Kate felt her heart sinking. She repeated her mother's words. "Go back to New York? Oh, no. Please . . ."

"Zoey, not right now. Later, okay?"

"No, Lucas, now. We have to talk." She stood directly in front of him. "Don't wriggle away, telling me you have to talk to relatives. You have days to talk to them. This can't wait." Now that she'd begun to speak, Zoey felt more comfortable with Lucas. He was the same old Lucas, no matter what happened. And his decision would be the right one. She sensed her parents watching her. They were waiting for his decision, too.

"Lucas, do you want me to stay?" It was as simple as that. She waited. Did he not understand? She sighed. "Lucas, do you want me—"

"Why the hell are you asking me this?" Lucas took her by the shoulders. "Zoey, my dad is dead. You won't help him by hanging around here, rotting. And I'm going to need help for a long time. Not just next week, or the week after, when everybody on Chatham Island is fussing over me. I need you later, when it really gets tough, when everybody forgets about it, when I start to forget my own father. That's when I'll need you." He looked into her eyes.

"Am I interrupting something?" Nina grinned at the two of them.

"No, we were just discussing Zoey's trip to Washington," Lucas said casually.

"Oh, so you're going, huh?" Nina asked.

Zoey nodded at Nina, but her smile was for Lucas. He'd given her a gift, a way out of her terrible dilemma. Though she knew it was costing him, Lucas had sacrificed for her. Of course he wanted her with him. How could she have doubted it? But he knew she had to go, and he also knew that she needed his support to go ahead with her trip.

Zoey looked from Nina to Lucas and back. They both smiled at her. "My best friends," Zoey breathed. "You two are my best friends."

"Hey, guys, mind if I snap a picture?" It was Zoey's dad. He motioned for the three of them to line up. At the last minute Zoey stepped out of the picture. She turned to look at Nina and Lucas. Nina was clowning around as usual, planting a kiss on Lucas's cheek, while Lucas tried to lift her off the ground. They looked like two puppies playing.

"Hey, Zo, why'd you step out of the picture?"

I don't know. I don't know why I stepped . . . out of the picture, Zoey thought. But aloud she said, "Take care of Lucas for me while I'm away." She looked into Nina's suddenly serious eyes. "Okay, Nina? Take care of Lucas for me."

Making Out: Trouble with Aaron

Book 21 in the explosive series about broken hearts, secrets, friendship, and of course, love.

Aaron was mad about **Zoey**, then he played around with **Kate** and now he's in love with **Claire**. Or is he? **Claire's** hurt so many people, especially **Jake** and **Lucas**. Now it looks as if she's next in line for a broken heart. The last thing **Claire** needs is . . .

Trouble with Aaron

READ ONE...READ THEM ALL—
The Hot New Series about Falling in Love

M A K I N G   O U T

by KATHERINE APPLEGATE

(#1) Zoey fools around   80211-2 /$3.99 US/$5.50 Can

(#2) Jake finds out   80212-0/$3.99 US/$4.99 Can

(#3) Nina won't tell   80213-9/$3.99 US/$4.99 Can

(#4) Ben's in love   80214-7/$3.99 US/$4.99 Can

(#5) Claire gets caught   80215-5/$3.99 US/$5.50 Can

(#6) What Zoey saw   80216-3/$3.99 US/$4.99 Can

(#7) Lucas gets hurt   80217-1 /$3.99 US/$4.99 Can

(#8) Aisha goes wild   80219-8/$3.99 US/$4.99 Can

(#9) Zoey plays games   80742-4/$3.99 US/$4.99 Can

(#10) Nina shapes up   80743-2/$3.99 US/$5.50 Can

(#11) Ben takes a chance   80867-6/$3.99 US/$5.50 Can

MAKING OUT

by KATHERINE APPLEGATE

(#12) Claire can't lose 80868-4/$3.99 US/$5.50 Can

(#13) Don't tell Zoey 80869-2/$3.99 US/$5.50 Can

(#14) Aaron lets go 80870-6/$3.99 US/$5.50 Can

(#15) Who loves Kate? 80871-4/$3.99 US/$5.50 Can

(#16) Lara gets even 80872-2/$3.99 US/$5.50 Can

(#17) Two-timing Aisha 81119-7/$3.99 US/$5.50 Can

(#18) Zoey speaks out 81120-0/$3.99 US/$5.99 Can

(#19) Kate finds love 81121-9/$3.99 US/$5.99 Can